'My brother

coop,'

Travis admitted. '

to. Or why.'

It was the last thing Rory expected to hear. The groom she'd flown all the way out here to marry was missing? 'I don't understand.' Her heart leapt into her throat, threatening to choke her.

Travis rested his arm along the open door of the truck. His expression held a trace of compassion, which only made Rory feel worse. The last thing she wanted was this man's pity.

'I'll take you to the airport,' he offered.

'I'm not leaving.'

Travis's eyes narrowed and he seemed to draw himself up even taller. 'I don't know when he'll be back,' he said.

Despite the tears of disappointment that threatened, she lifted her chin and gritted her teeth. 'I'll wait.' If this man thought he was going to intimidate her, he had another think coming…

Dear Reader

Welcome to this month's fantastic line-up from Special Edition™. In *Older, Wiser...Pregnant*, the latest THAT'S MY BABY! title, Laurel Cameron returns to her home town and her first love, but will Beau Walker accept her when he finds out she's carrying another man's child?

Meanwhile, Travis Winchester is in big trouble in Pamela Toth's *The Mail-Order Mix-Up*, he's met the woman of his dreams, but she's his *brother's* mail-order bride! And don't miss the latest instalment of Victoria Pade's A RANCHING FAMILY series, where Yance Culhane unexpectedly finds an instant family.

Cathy Gillen Thacker's back this month, too, with the second in her trilogy and an absolute delight! An unlikely couple turn up the heat, oblivious to the blizzard raging outside their door…

Finally this month, will love conquer all? Find out in *Meant To Be Married* where lovers have to contend with their families' ill-will before they can wed. And it's a case of opposites attract when Jillian Marshall decides to become *The Bodyguard's Bride*.

Happy reading

The Editors.

The Mail-Order Mix-Up

PAMELA TOTH

First published in Great Britain 1999
Silhouette Books, Eton House, 18-24 Paradise Road,
Richmond, Surrey TW9 1SR

ISBN 0 373 24197 6

23-9905

Printed and bound in Spain
by Litografía Rosés S.A., Barcelona

PAMELA TOTH

was born in Wisconsin, but grew up in Seattle, where she attended the University of Washington and graduated in art. She still lives near Seattle, and she has two daughters, and several Siamese cats. When she isn't writing, she enjoys reading, travelling, quilting and researching new story ideas.

She loves hearing from readers, and can be reached at P.O. Box 5845, Bellevue, WA 98006, U.S.A. For a personal reply, a self-addressed envelope with return postage is appreciated.

Other novels by Pamela Toth

Silhouette Special Edition®

Thunderstruck
Dark Angel
Old Enough To Know Better
Two Sets of Footprints
A Warming Trend
Walk Away, Joe
The Wedding Knot
Rocky Mountain Rancher
Buchanan's Bride
Buchanan's Baby
Buchanan's Return
The Paternity Test

To my daughter Erika, one of the brightest lights
in my life.
And to Frank, keeper of my heart.

Chapter One

Rory Mancini hesitated on the bottom step of the bus that had brought her to Waterloo, Colorado, and gazed hopefully at the three old cowboys sprawled in wooden chairs in front of the post office, sunning themselves like lizards on a flat rock. They stared back at her with open curiosity, but none of them rose to greet her.

Outside the cocoon of the air-conditioned bus, the afternoon sun beat down on Rory's unprotected head and soaked through the wool of her tweed blazer. Perspiration beaded her upper lip.

She glanced up and down the quaint wooden sidewalk, but she didn't see anyone who resembled the snapshot Charlie Winchester had sent her. She'd flown halfway across the country and he had promised to meet her, but maybe Charlie was running late.

Rory's mouth was dry, but she wasn't sure if it was thirst or nerves. Either way, perhaps she had time to find a cool drink before he showed up.

Another passenger spoke from behind her. "Excuse me, but if you aren't getting off here, would you mind letting me by?"

"I'm sorry." Hastily, Rory clutched her shoulder bag and stepped down onto the platform. Her new boots pinched her toes. She supposed the heat and the long ride from the airport had made her feet swell.

Rory pushed her sunglasses back up her nose and studied her surroundings. Nothing in her experience had prepared her for Waterloo. Charlie had warned her it was small, but Rory had grown up in the Big Apple. Small could mean just about anything.

The main street looked like the set from an old Western movie, its row of false-fronted buildings as sun-baked as the trio sitting on the post office porch. An ancient pickup truck passed slowly, towing a dusty horse trailer. Rory's heart leaped, and then she saw that the driver was a woman. Several other trucks and one car were parked along the street, but the sidewalk was empty.

Rory wouldn't have been surprised to see a man bolt from the brick-faced bank, guns blazing and a bandanna covering half his face. Instead, the only thing moving was the bus driver, who had climbed down to open the luggage compartment.

He looked up at Rory expectantly.

"Those two blue ones are mine," she told him, pointing to the old-fashioned suitcases she'd bought from a neighbor back in the Bronx. Had it only been a week ago that she'd decided to come to Colorado?

"Anything else?" the driver asked as he set the bags in front of her.

"No, thanks."

He glanced around the empty street. "Someone coming to meet you?"

Rory nodded, wondering how he could tell she wasn't a native. Her boots were Western, and she was wearing silver earrings she'd bought at the Denver airport. They were shaped like tiny sheriff's badges. Perhaps she should have bought a hat, instead, to shield her from the sun. "He must be running late," she replied. No doubt the heat had turned her complexion a bright pink.

"We were a little early." The driver glanced at the gray tweed jacket she wore over a black camisole top. "You can wait across the street at the café," he suggested. "It may not have air-conditioning, but you'll be out of the sun."

After Rory thanked him again, he climbed back into the bus and shut the door behind him. For one wild moment, she was tempted to demand that he take her back to Denver. Only her own stubborn pride and the realization that there was nothing left for her in New York kept her from doing so. Before she could sort through her mixed feelings, the air brakes on the bus belched and it rumbled into the street.

Feeling as if she'd just lost her last friend, Rory lifted her curly red hair off her nape and flapped the open edge of her jacket back and forth in a vain attempt to cool herself. Even the faint breeze was warm, and the vigorous movement made her hotter.

She was about to pick up her suitcases and cross the street to the café when she noticed another dusty pickup coming toward her. Immediately, butterflies the size of small bats began swooping and diving in her stomach. She licked her lips and resisted the urge to fluff up her hair. Was she finally going to meet the man she'd been corresponding with for the last four months?

As Travis Winchester parked his truck, he saw the bus pull out. A tall redhead was standing alone in front of the post office with a couple of suitcases. There was no doubt she was the one he was here for.

Travis would have liked to wring his younger brother's neck for what he'd done—leaving a note under Travis's door while he was asleep and then slinking off like a dog. With the fall roundup starting in a couple of days and the ranch cook called out of town on an emergency, this little chore was the last thing Travis needed.

For a moment, he was tempted to turn around and drive back out of town. It wasn't his fault Charlie had gotten cold feet. Perhaps when no one showed up to meet her, the redhead would just take the next bus back to Denver.

Unfortunately for all of them, the next bus didn't come for two days. If the woman was desperate enough to travel all this way just to see Charlie, what were the chances she'd have the money to go back where she'd come from?

Abandoning her without knowing was more than Travis could do. With a sigh of resignation, he switched off the engine and opened his door.

He didn't need this, he thought. What he needed was a cook.

The woman was watching him walk toward her. To his intense displeasure, he saw that the old men who hung around the post office were watching him, too. Heat swept up Travis's neck. He hated being the center of attention.

His gaze shifted back to the woman. Despite her conservative outfit, her height and coloring would have made her stand out in a Broadway chorus line. Her mass of coppery hair glowed in the bright sunlight as if it were on fire. Dark glasses hid her eyes, but her cheeks bloomed with color. She was tall for a woman and her back was ramrod straight. Even dressed as she was in a tailored jacket and black jeans that hugged her long legs, she was a little too flashy for Travis's taste.

"Are you Aurora Mancini?" he asked when he was close enough to speak without raising his voice. He pronounced the unusual name carefully. With a handle like that, perhaps she *was* some kind of entertainer. Charlie's note had been painfully brief, and Travis hadn't known before today that he'd been writing to anyone.

She flashed him a fifty-megawatt smile. "Charlie? You aren't what I pictured." She thrust out her hands and Travis took a hasty step back.

At his inadvertent reaction, her smile faltered and she dropped her arms.

"I'm sorry," she said quickly, cheeks growing pinker, "I didn't mean I was disappointed. It's just that the photo you sent didn't really show your face. I don't remember the mustache. The brim of your hat cast a shadow...." Her voice trailed off, as if she realized she was chattering, and she pushed her sunglasses up off her face. "I just meant that I had no idea what you looked like."

Travis hadn't said a word. He was too busy recovering from the sudden onslaught of her femininity on his sex-starved senses. He was a tall man, but he only had to bend his head slightly to gaze right into her eyes, which were a deep, velvety blue. He sucked in a breath, and her perfume, a tantalizing blend of subtlety and sin, wrapped around his brain like nerve gas. The husky edge to her voice was a promise in itself. Only a small bump on her nose and a dusting of freckles kept her from being too perfect.

While he struggled with his reaction, her gaze met his squarely. If she was exhausted from the trip and drooping from the heat in that heavy jacket, she hid it well.

"Perhaps we should start over," she suggested. "Hi, Charlie."

With no little effort, Travis unstuck his tongue from the roof of his mouth where it had plastered itself and cleared his throat.

"I'm not Charlie," he replied.

Her mouth, as inviting as peach ice cream, fell open. "You're not?" She glanced past him, as if she expected Charlie to spring up from the dust of the street. "Where is he?"

Abruptly, she paled and clutched at his arm. Her eyes widened. "Oh, dear, he didn't get hurt, did he? I've heard that working on a ranch can be so dangerous."

Travis pictured what he would like to do to Charlie when he caught up with the little weasel. Ranch work could be *very* dangerous indeed. "No, ma'am. He's not hurt.'' *Not yet,* he added silently. Charlie had screwed up in the past, but this was a new low.

Her shoulders slumped with relief. The hand that gripped his forearm let go and fluttered to her chest. An impressive chest, Travis noticed as he glimpsed something black and lacy in the open vee of her jacket.

''Did something come up at the last minute?'' she asked. ''I mean, he did persuade me to come. He even sent my ticket. If this isn't a good time…'' Again her voice trailed away, as if she realized the impracticality of what she'd been about to suggest. She'd flown all the way from New York City. It wasn't as if she could turn around and come back later.

Even though Travis wished like hell she could—sometime when *he* wasn't the one who would have to deal with her.

A drop of perspiration trickled from her hairline down the side of her face. Guilt stabbed him. The least he could do was to suggest they move into the shade. He glanced across the street, reluctant to draw any more attention than the old busybodies on the porch were already giving them.

It couldn't be helped. Travis hated being the object of town gossip and speculation almost as much as he hated having to deal with Aurora Mancini in the first place, but his innate sense of decency wouldn't allow him to keep her standing in the sun while he figured out what to do with her.

''Would you like something cold to drink?'' he asked abruptly. ''We could go over to Emma's.'' He eyed her heightened color with growing concern.

"Frankly, you look like you could use some iced tea."

When she wiped away the trickle of perspiration, Travis was surprised to see that her nails were short and unpolished. He would have expected them to be long, lethal and brightly colored, since his imagination persisted in painting her as some exotic creature, awash in sequins and trailing a feather stole. Wearing high heels instead of boots. Brand-new boots, he noticed, wondering if they'd given her blisters yet.

In reality, he had no idea what she did when she wasn't stalking someone like his brother. Charlie had only given him her name and the time of her arrival from New York. He hadn't even said where he was going, just that he had lost his nerve and was heading for parts unknown until the dust settled, she was gone and it was safe for him to come home.

Funny, Travis mused, meeting women had never been a problem for his outgoing brother. He muttered an exasperated curse under his breath.

"I'm sorry?" Her eyes widened.

This was going nearly as badly as it possibly could. All he needed to make his day complete was for her to collapse in the street with heat exhaustion, duly documented by the mangy old coots who were watching their every move.

Automatically, he reached for her elbow to escort her to Emma's. "Leave your bags here. They'll be okay until we get back."

To his surprise, she resisted. "Not until you tell me who you are and what you've done with Charlie Winchester."

Hell's bells, Travis thought. Was she afraid he was

going to abduct her? Toss her over his shoulder, run to his truck and tear out of town in a cloud of dust in front of witnesses? Was that the way they did things where she came from?

Abruptly, he realized it was probably a regular occurrence in New York. This, however, was rural Colorado, where the arrival of a stranger was news—especially if she had red hair and the most kissable mouth he'd seen in way too long.

"I'm Travis Winchester, Charlie's older brother," he explained belatedly. "Maybe he mentioned me."

Her expression cleared, and her lips, looking moist despite the dry heat, relaxed into that lethal smile. "Of course. He wrote all about both you and Adam. I'm pleased to meet you." She glanced down, but his hand stayed at his side.

What had Charlie told her? It didn't matter. Travis was quickly losing patience with the whole situation. If Charlie had wanted this woman to have a warm Colorado welcome, he should have come himself. Travis had more pressing matters to deal with. Especially when he really had no idea what was going on. He was getting hot himself, standing here in the sun, and he was wasting valuable time—time he should be spending in search of a cook and dealing with a hundred other details of the roundup to come.

"Anyway, Charlie wasn't able to be here," he said bluntly. At her continued stare, he blew out an exasperated breath. "I mean, he's gone. He's asked me to meet you in his place."

"Gone?" she echoed. "Gone where?" Her voice rose slightly, and perspiration beaded her upper lip, pooling in the tasty-looking dip above the bow. "He knew I was coming today."

As he looked away from the concern and puzzlement on her face, Travis removed his hat and whacked it against his thigh. He'd rather be picking ticks off a rabid dog than dealing with Miss Mancini. He raked his hand through his hair. Sweat gathered under his arms. From the trio of old men he heard a loud guffaw, as if they were amusing themselves by speculating on his private conversation. No doubt they could tell from his body language that things weren't going well.

Tugging his hat back onto his head, Travis gazed up at the intense blue of the sky and considered the situation. "I'm not going into it here," he said. "If you want to know anything more about my baby brother, you'll have to come over to the café." With that, he whirled on his heel and walked away without a backward glance, ignoring her squawk of protest.

Rory watched him retreat, his loose-hipped walk snagging her attention despite her confusion and irritation. Why had Charlie sent his brother to meet her instead of coming himself? She thought she knew Charlie from his letters. Would have bet her future he had character.

Rory swallowed the sudden lump in her throat as she realized that was exactly what she'd done. Glancing both ways, she limped after Travis, determined to demand he tell her what was going on.

Despite the way her boots were pinching, she caught up with him at the door to the café, a skinny, painted wooden building like the others that lined the street. Emma's was distinguished from its neighbors only by the sign swinging over the sidewalk and the faded red-and-white checkered curtains hanging limply at the windows.

As if he knew she would follow him, Travis opened the door and stepped aside without even glancing back over his broad shoulder. Rory was five-eleven in bare feet, and she wasn't used to having men tower over her, but Travis made her feel ridiculously petite. She dragged in a long breath and went inside.

As she did, she barely noticed that conversation in the café stopped as suddenly as if someone had thrown a switch. It *was* cooler in here, and the place smelled divine. A distinct rumble from her stomach reminded her that she hadn't eaten anything since the night before except the airline's idea of a breakfast burrito. There hadn't been time to grab lunch before boarding the bus from the airport and now she was paying for it. The aromas wafting from the kitchen behind the long counter were making her light-headed.

She swayed, almost grateful when Travis's fingers clasped her upper arm.

"Are you okay?" He was looking down at her with apparent concern on his roughly attractive face.

Rory willed herself to square her shoulders and lift her chin. "Of course."

His frown lessened and he released her with unflattering haste. Her stomach let out another determined grumble and her knees wobbled. She'd been foolish not to carry some kind of snack in her purse, but she refused to show any sign of weakness in front of this man.

Rory had the distinct impression that he didn't like her very much. What she didn't understand was why. They'd barely met. Charlie certainly hadn't hinted at any problems in his letters.

Almost before she realized what he was doing, Travis dragged a chair back from a table and thrust her into it. "Hazel, would you bring a glass of iced tea right away?" he asked in a commanding voice.

The waitress he'd addressed by name hurried to comply. Before Rory could ask him any of the questions buzzing in her brain like drunken bees, a tall, sweating glass filled with tea, ice and a bright yellow lemon wedge was plunked down in front of her.

"Drink this, honey. You look parched," said a round-faced woman wearing an old-fashioned hairnet and a pink nylon uniform.

Gratefully, Rory complied, thanking her after she'd taken a long swallow, but doing her best to ignore the man who sat across from her.

After Hazel had apparently satisfied herself that Rory wasn't going to keel over, she slid a menu in front of her and handed one to Travis.

"The soup today is navy bean," she said before bustling away.

Rory couldn't imagine anything worse than hot soup on a day like this.

"Bring her a bowl," Travis called after the waitress.

Rory opened her mouth to protest, met the intense expression in his charcoal eyes head-on, and instead clamped her lips around the straw in her glass of iced tea. She wasn't up to explaining that she had no use for a man with a control complex; she needed to save her strength for something really important. When the soup came, she just wouldn't eat it.

After she'd taken another bracing swallow of tea, she looked up again. This time she found herself hoping that Charlie resembled his brother in appearance—and didn't in personality.

Back on the street, when Travis had removed his hat, she had seen that his hair was the same warm medium brown as his mustache. He looked more approachable without the Stetson he was wearing now as he watched her, face expressionless. Even his eyes were unreadable.

As the silence between them lengthened, Rory glanced around. The street had been deserted, but the little café was fairly crowded. The chorus of voices rose and fell against the commingled background noise of country music from a radio on the counter and the clatter of dishes from the kitchen. No one appeared to be taking any further notice of Rory.

The popularity of nonsmoking establishments must not have made its way to Waterloo yet; the smoke from several cigarettes rose like cobras from a snake charmer's basket. Travis's shirt pockets were empty; before Rory could ask if he or Charlie smoked, Hazel returned with a large bowl of soup, setting it and a basket of crackers in front of her. The aroma made her swallow thickly.

''Anything else?'' Hazel asked. Rory glanced up, but the question had been directed at Travis.

''Bring me a burger, would you? A side of fries and coffee.'' He looked over at Rory, and the ghost of a smile flickered across his lean face.

She followed the direction of his amused gaze until

she was staring at the full soup spoon poised in her hand. Hastily, she put it back down. Again her stomach emitted a loud rumble.

"Don't wait for me," he drawled. "Eat up. We'll talk afterward."

Deciding that pride only went so far, Rory did just that.

Between bites of his hamburger, Travis watched her devour the whole bowl of soup and half the basket of crackers. Once she began eating, she hadn't raised her head. Nothing wrong with her appetite, he thought, and then he wondered how long it had been since her last meal.

"Anything else?" he asked when she finally laid down her spoon and looked up.

With a contented sigh, she shook her head as she sat back and took a long drink of her iced tea. "No, thank you."

"Not even pie?" he asked with a quirk of his brow. "It's homemade by Emma herself."

She hesitated, nibbling her lip, and he found himself swallowing a chuckle. At least she didn't pick at her food like some women. Not that his experience with the opposite sex had been all that extensive, but the ones he had been around seemed to think a hearty appetite was somehow unfeminine.

When Hazel came back to collect their empty dishes, Travis ordered two pieces of apple pie and ice cream.

"Did you want coffee, Aurora?" he asked when her head snapped up. She'd been staring at her bowl as if she'd expected Charlie to appear there. The thought made him frown with displeasure.

"Call me Rory," she corrected him.

"Rory," he echoed, relieved. Not that it mattered, but he couldn't see himself calling her Aurora for even the brief time she would be here. It was the name of a nearby town, not a woman who looked like a showgirl.

Suddenly Travis realized he should have called the airlines already to make her return reservation. The airport was only about a two-hour drive away and he'd take her there himself.

"Apple pie is fine," she said quietly, addressing Hazel. "But no coffee or ice cream, thank you."

Travis had known Hazel since he'd been in grade school, and he could almost feel her curiosity. It wasn't every day he brought a woman into Emma's, especially one who looked like Rory. To her credit, Hazel merely nodded in acknowledgment of the order and left with their empty dishes.

As soon as she was out of earshot, Rory stared at Travis expectantly. "So," she said, gripping the edge of the table, "tell me what happened to Charlie."

Travis glanced around to see if anyone else was likely to overhear their conversation. No one was paying them the slightest attention now.

He wondered whether Rory was likely to make a scene when he explained the situation, and he seriously considered stalling until they were out of the busy café. But, if he had any hopes of getting her on a return flight today, he had to tell her something.

Deliberately, Travis leaned forward on his folded

arms and lowered his voice. With a frown of concentration, Rory did the same.

''There's a problem,'' he began, ignoring the way her mouth tightened at his words. ''I'd really rather not go into it here. If you'd just wait until we're done with our pie—''

''If there's some kind of problem with Charlie, I think I have a right to know,'' she interrupted. ''You said he was okay, that nothing has happened to him, but he was supposed to be here and I sure don't see him. So what's going on?''

Travis glanced out the window at her suitcases still sitting across the street where they had left them. He didn't know how best to proceed. He wasn't used to a woman being so forceful and overriding him like this. Hell, he wasn't too used to women, period. His mother had left when he was eight. Sure, other women had drifted in and out of his life since then—an aunt, teachers, a few girlfriends in school and a couple more serious relationships afterward, but no one for a while now and none he'd been really close to in an emotional way. He supposed that was his fault. For the last few years, the only woman in the family had been his older brother Adam's wife, but she was no longer around, either.

He pinched the bridge of his nose between two fingers. The Winchester men didn't have a lot of luck with women, he mused. As he sipped his cooling coffee, Rory watched him. Then Hazel bustled back, balancing two plates of pie in one hand and a full coffeepot in the other. Travis breathed a sigh of relief at the reprieve.

"Want more iced tea, honey?" Hazel asked Rory as she topped off Travis's cup.

She shook her head with a muttered thanks, barely taking her gaze from his. He could tell she was impatient with the interruption, but he dug into his pie à la mode with more enthusiasm than he felt. Hazel tore their check off her pad and set it near his plate.

"Have a nice afternoon," she said cheerfully. "And come back real soon."

Watching Travis eat, Rory did her best to hold back the unease that was beginning to test her already overburdened composure. The last few weeks had been difficult for her, starting with the unexpected loss of her job and culminating with the traumatic events that prompted her decision to come here. The soup she'd eaten had restored her temporarily, but it was no magic elixir. She'd expected to be met by someone she had established a certain bond with, a sense of trust that had grown over the course of their correspondence. Charlie might still be a stranger in some ways, but in others she felt she knew him very well.

Instead, she was sharing a table with a man who, under different circumstances, would have put all her girlish instincts on red alert—a brooding male who some of her friends back home would have labeled, without any hesitation, an out-and-out "hunk." One who was obviously unimpressed by her modest charms and whom she suspected was less than happy to be here. Neither did he appear any too eager to enlighten her about the whereabouts of his brother.

Concern was putting Rory's senses on a red alert of a different kind. Worry threatened, and close behind it, panic was starting to chew at the ragged edges of her emotional equilibrium.

Suddenly unwilling to wait for another moment, she reached over and plucked Travis's fork from his unresisting fingers as it descended back toward his pie.

"I want to know what's going on, and I want to know now," she said quietly, holding the fork hostage.

The expression on his face was almost comical, his Adam's apple bobbing as he swallowed the last bite he'd taken. Apparently he wasn't used to anyone usurping either his authority or his eating utensils.

For a long moment, they stared at each other. Then he cleared his throat.

"You said earlier that you have a right to know," he began. "Perhaps you do, since my brother obviously invited you here, but I'm not sure just why he did, or why you came. It's obvious the two of you have never even met."

Rory appeared to hesitate. "It's true we've never actually met," she said, "but your brother and I are planning to be married."

Chapter Two

Was *this* what Charlie had been referring to when he'd written that he'd gotten cold feet—a mail-order bride? Travis could scarcely believe his ears. "That's the most preposterous thing I've ever heard."

Rearing back in his chair, he glanced around the café. His outburst had attracted the attention of several other customers, including a teller from the local bank who belonged both to his church and the women's quilting group. When he met her inquisitive glance with a black glare, she quickly averted her face.

It was bad enough for Charlie to run out on a guest, but the idea that he would consider marriage without saying anything to his own brother was downright painful for Travis to swallow.

Briefly, he wondered whether Adam knew. He'd

already been gone this morning when Travis found Charlie's note. Would Charlie have confided in their elder brother and not Travis?

When the three of them were growing up, Charlie had gotten into one scrape after another, but never anything really serious—and nothing as irresponsible as running out on his bride-to-be.

Travis might have doubted Rory's claim, except for the fact she had no idea he couldn't pick up a phone and check it out. Damn. If only he knew where Charlie was hiding.

Hands folded in front of her, Rory was waiting with a calmness betrayed only by the color staining her cheeks. "Preposterous or not, I'm telling the truth," she said quietly.

Travis wondered how much of his frustration was due to his own gut reaction to her announcement. As much as he would have liked to deny it, the image of Charlie claiming her as his bride seared through Travis like acid. He was jealous of his own brother.

Rory Mancini was as out of place here as an orchid in a cactus patch—in this café, in this town and in Travis's life. He'd better damn well remember it or things were going from bad to worse quicker than a weather change in Denver.

One more reason to hustle her onto the first plane out of Colorado. If Charlie didn't like it, too bad.

"Let's go," Travis told her, shaking off his conflicting emotions. "It's time we had a serious discussion, and I'd prefer it to be anywhere but here."

"Where are you taking me?" At least there was no wariness in her midnight blue eyes this time, but neither had she gotten compliantly to her feet.

Travis considered quickly. ''We can talk in the truck.'' Eager to escape their audience, he led the way outside and started back across the street.

Rory followed him in silence as they went to get her bags. She found the fact that no one had made off with them as quaint as the hitching rail along the sidewalk.

Her feet were still sore, but she did her best to keep up with Travis's ground-eating stride. When she lagged behind despite her efforts to hurry, he finally glanced over his shoulder. Then, with an impatient frown, he stopped and waited for her.

''New boots?'' he asked.

She nodded. ''My feet must have swollen on the plane.''

His eyebrows quirked. ''You didn't buy them here?''

''New York,'' she admitted.

The corners of his mouth twitched. ''Ah, the hub of the Western boot market.''

For a moment, Rory was tempted to chuckle. Then she realized he was merely trying to distract her. He still hadn't told her about Charlie.

''Is that your truck?'' She nodded toward a black pickup covered with dust.

''Yeah. Can you walk or would you like me to carry you? I'll come back for your suitcases.''

Despite the heat, a shiver of awareness tingled down Rory's spine like the touch of ghostly fingers. Needing some protection from the intensity of his gaze, she reached for the sunglasses she'd pushed up to the top of her head.

''Leave them be,'' Travis said, watching her.

Rory hesitated. Then, with a patently careless shrug, she complied. ''I can walk.'' Even if she had to walk on razor blades, she vowed silently. And that was just what each step felt like, but she wouldn't have admitted it to the man at her side. Instead, she breathed a sigh of relief when they reached the truck and he hefted her bags into the back.

''How far is the ranch?'' she asked as he held open the door for her. Something in the way he didn't quite meet her gaze aroused her suspicions. ''You are taking me to the ranch, aren't you?''

After a nearly imperceptible pause, he shook his head. ''We're going to the airport.''

Rory felt as though she'd been sucker punched. ''Why? What's happened to Charlie?''

Travis didn't answer.

''I'm not going anywhere until you tell me.'' Rory folded her arms across her chest and leaned against the truck, ignoring the dust. Despite the food and iced tea, she was tired. It had already been a long day, one that threatened to grow painfully longer before it was over, but she wasn't going back.

While she waited for Travis to speak, two teenage boys and a girl with long hair walked by. They all wore cowboy hats, T-shirts and jeans, but the noise coming from the ghetto blaster one carried sounded just like the music kids were listening to back in New York. The girl glanced at Rory, smiled shyly when their eyes met and then looked away. Somehow the moment of human contact warmed her, gave her courage.

As soon as the young people were out of hearing range, Travis cleared his throat. ''Charlie flew the coop,'' he admitted. ''I have no idea where he's gone off to, or why.''

It was the last thing she expected to hear. ''I don't understand.'' Her lips felt numb and rubbery, as if they'd been injected with Novocain. Her heart leaped into her throat and was stuck there, threatening to choke her. Her knees had turned to water. She'd thought that Charlie, unlike her jerk of an ex-husband, was someone she could count on.

Travis rested his arm along the open door of the truck. His expression bore a trace of compassion, which only made Rory feel worse. The last thing she wanted was this man's pity. She didn't question why. Instead, she started to tell him she would find her own way back to Denver, and then she remembered her financial situation.

''Charlie was the one who brought me out here,'' she insisted as she struggled not to cry, ''and Charlie is the one who will have to tell me to go home. Until that happens, I'm not leaving.''

Travis's eyes narrowed and he seemed to draw himself up even taller. Was it only Rory's imagination that his shoulders blocked out the sun? ''I don't know when he'll be back,'' he said.

Despite the tears of disappointment that threatened, she lifted her chin and gritted her teeth. If this cowboy thought he was going to intimidate her, he had another think coming. ''I'll wait.''

He blinked. Then he shoved back his hat and looked around. ''Where do you intend to do that? The only motel in Waterloo isn't fit for livestock, and last I heard, the two boardinghouses were full up with the construction crew working on the new overpass outside town.''

He was probably telling the truth. Rory sure hadn't noticed a popular hotel chain poking up anywhere. It looked as though she was stuck, out of options and very nearly out of money as well, but she wasn't about to admit it—not to Travis.

''What ever happened to that famous western hospitality we easterners keep hearing about?'' she drawled as she peered up at him through her lashes. It was the kind of gesture she despised in other women, but desperate times called for desperate measures. ''If I'd thought Charlie was the kind of guy who was going to bail out on me, I wouldn't have come all this way to see him.''

''Charlie didn't bail out on you,'' Travis began angrily, only to stop and ball his fists at his sides in obvious frustration. It was beginning to look as if that was exactly what Charlie had done.

Rory merely lifted her eyebrows, although she was trembling inside. ''I can wait at his place,'' she suggested airily, hoping Travis couldn't hear her heart thudding. Charlie had written that he lived at the ranch.

''No way.'' Travis was shaking his head before she'd finished speaking. ''That's not a good idea.''

''Why not? He did invite me.''

''And you were going to stay with him?''

She glanced away, embarrassed. ''We're getting married,'' she reminded him.

''In the light of what's happened, you may have to put those plans on hold,'' he pointed out dryly. ''The groom seems to be missing.''

''The bride still needs a place to stay,'' she snapped, a headache beginning behind her eyes.

Travis appeared to reconsider. She held her breath.

''Perhaps we'd better go to Charlie's place and sort this out there,'' he said gruffly. Then he gripped her elbow and all but pitched her into the truck.

Before he'd shut her door and circled the cab, Rory's sudden burst of relief at his capitulation was already fading. Getting information from Travis was like finding a cab during rush hour in a rainstorm.

Oh, dear. Charlie wasn't already married, was he? Surely Travis wouldn't be so mean as to take her to meet his brother's *wife,* for pity's sake.

Nervously, she watched Travis back out of the parking spot, but she couldn't bring herself to ask. Instead, she did her best to curb her impatience and wait for him to speak.

Travis maintained a grim silence as they left town in the opposite direction from which the bus had come. Ahead of them the land stretched as flat as day-old soda, empty but for an occasional cluster of buildings or a line of fence. The straight two-lane road ran all the way to the horizon. Despite all her misgivings, Rory felt herself being filled with a soaring sense of adventure as big as the blue sky overhead.

Travis drove with one hand as he dug into his shirt pocket with the other. ''This was under my door when I got up this morning,'' he said, passing her a folded piece of paper.

As soon as she opened it up, Rory recognized Charlie's handwriting. Dread welled inside her. She started reading, and the knot of anxiety that had been forming in her stomach suddenly doubled in size and squeezed tight.

"Why would he do this?" she whispered, crumpling the note into a ball.

Travis glanced at her, one hand on the wheel and the other rubbing his jaw. "I was hoping you'd tell me."

Rory stared at his profile. "W-what do you mean?"

He shrugged. "Did you have a disagreement? A misunderstanding?"

Slowly, she shook her head. "He called yesterday. It was the first time I talked to him on the phone." Bitterly, she recalled how reassured she'd been by his warm, easy drawl. Didn't she ever learn?

She dragged her attention back to the matter at hand. "Nothing was wrong," she insisted, even as her brain was asking, Why, why? "He sounded fine. He said he'd be here. I offered to call from the airport, but he told me that wasn't necessary." She didn't understand what was happening.

"*Something* was wrong," Travis corrected her, slapping his hand against the wheel. "It's not like Charlie to run out on his responsibilities."

Rory frowned. His responsibility. That hurt. And didn't it make her sound like a burden?

One Travis clearly didn't want.

She'd been right to not be entirely honest with him. Oh, it was true that she had answered Charlie's ad for a mail-order bride, even if it had been on a whim. As the long, stifling New York summer crawled by, his letters had been like a refreshing breeze in her life. She treasured their growing friendship. Then disaster struck, and his suggestion that she come to Colorado, no obligation, had been a lifeline she'd grabbed out of sheer desperation.

But she couldn't imagine agreeing to marry a man she'd never met, and she'd made her feelings plain. Charlie hadn't objected.

So why had she told Travis just the opposite? To shock him? To protect herself from the reluctant attraction she felt toward him by declaring herself unavailable?

One look at the forbidding expression on his face and she realized she had nothing to worry about in that department. But now it was too late to confess without looking like a fool and a liar. Silently, she handed back Charlie's crumpled note.

"Now you know at least as much as I do," he said, stuffing it in his pocket.

She didn't bother to respond. What could she say? She really didn't have any idea why Charlie had left. Especially since he *wasn't* running from an unwelcome bride-to-be.

After a few more minutes of silence, Travis turned off the main road and drove through an open gate with The Running W Ranch painted on a wooden sign in neat black letters. "I don't know why you want to wait for him. We have no idea when he'll show up."

Rory didn't look at Travis as he braked. What she wanted wasn't at issue. Necessity dictated that she hang around when pride would have urged her to wish Charlie Winchester and his arrogant brother to a darker, hotter place and then wing her way back home. "I'll wait," she said firmly.

Stubborn or desperate? Travis wondered as he drove over the cattle guard. Couldn't she take a hint?

It was obvious that Charlie didn't want her here, and neither did he. He would have liked to tell her as much, but the words wouldn't come out. He shouldn't feel responsible for her, but the truth was, he did. Charlie was his brother. Until he decided to put in an appearance, Travis felt honor-bound to keep an eye on her.

A very close eye, a little voice inside his head jeered as he headed toward the main house. Rory's head swiveled back and forth as if she were trying to take in everything around them. They passed the turnoff to the fancy showplace Adam had built on a nearby rise when he got married just over a decade before. Now he lived there with his little girl and a full-time housekeeper. Hadn't Charlie learned anything from *Adam's* city woman about their sticking power?

"What a lovely house," Rory exclaimed, pointing to the dwelling surrounded by a stand of cottonwoods. "Who lives there?"

"Our brother Adam."

"Charlie wrote me about him," she said. "He sounds nice."

Nice? Yeah, Travis supposed she was right. Adam was steady and even-tempered. He'd shouldered responsibility for the ranch at a young age and now he was raising his daughter. Did that make him nice? He did what he had to, just as they all did.

Briefly, Travis considered taking Rory to Adam's, but then he discarded the idea. Despite her brave words, she wasn't going to be around long; no point in disrupting his brother's household any more than it already was—or in making her too comfortable.

He refused to consider that there might be another,

more selfish reason for his decision. Instead, he tried to anticipate her reaction to the house where he'd grown up.

What had Charlie told her about the spread? Did she expect something fancy, like a dude ranch? Did she think they were rich?

Well, he supposed they were, at least on paper. After their mother had walked out on them, their father's whole purpose in life had been making the ranch a success. From Travis's point of view, it was the one thing their old man had done right. Since Adam had taken it over, with his brothers' help and hard work, it had grown even bigger and more productive.

"The land around here seems so big and empty," Rory said, breaking into his thoughts.

He grunted noncommittally as they bounced down the rutted road. Was she probing, trying to find out the size of their holdings, or was it an understandable comment from someone who was used to tall buildings that blotted out the sky?

As they drove, Rory looked in every direction. "Where are the cattle?" she finally asked.

Travis pointed vaguely toward the horizon ahead. "Up that way. We'll start bringing them closer in the day after tomorrow. Fall roundup starts then." He remembered the missing cook and bit back an oath. Any chance the woman sitting beside him knew one end of a fry pan from the other? Probably not well enough to keep a dozen hardworking, hungry cowhands well fed and happy.

As always when Travis first glimpsed the old-fashioned two-story farmhouse where he had grown up, he was assaulted with mixed feelings. Theirs hadn't been a happy home, especially after his mother left. Lord, how he had missed her. He'd been eight years old, and he'd waited for a long time for her to come back, but she never had.

Travis and his brothers had tried hard to please their remaining parent, terrified that he, too, would abandon them. No matter what they did, though, it was never enough. To three scared little boys the ranch was a rival they couldn't compete with. Now the three of them were running it together, a legacy of dust and blood and sweat.

Blinking, he shook off the recollection.

"The house looks as if it's been here forever," Rory murmured.

Travis glanced at her sharply. Sure, the old homestead was a little run-down, but the daily chores took up nearly all of his time. "My father built this house," he replied, bristling as he parked near the back door. "It's solid, it's comfortable and it's plenty cozy in the wintertime."

When he would have climbed down from the cab, Rory reached out and touched his arm. Through the cotton of his shirt, he felt the fleeting contact like the heated kiss of a branding iron.

"I didn't mean to sound critical." Her expression was anxious. "The house looks as though it belongs here, in this setting. That's all I meant."

Impatiently, he shook off his reaction as he shook off her hand. "No problem," he growled, following the direction of her gaze. The house was a tall rectangle, with windows randomly cut into its clapboard walls, a stone chimney running up one side and, tacked onto the other, a single-story addition that served as an office. A wide porch stretched across the back, and Charlie had added a hot tub last summer. Travis seldom had the time to use it.

"Is this where Charlie lives?" Rory asked, opening her door and climbing down before Travis could make it around the truck to assist her.

He watched her face carefully. "Charlie and I both live here."

"Oh." Her mouth puckered with surprise. Without the peach lipstick, which had long since worn off, her lips looked as soft as the muzzle of a newborn colt.

With an effort, Travis jerked his attention from her mouth and their gazes collided. A frown pleated her forehead. He would have given a lot to know what she was thinking.

"Do you live right smack in New York City?" he asked, needing to know some little thing about her. Needing to break the sudden tension that had sprung up between them.

Her eyes misted over. "Mm-hm. The Bronx." She must have realized her reply told a Colorado boy nothing. "I had an apartment a few blocks from work," she added. "It's a real homey neighborhood."

Although he'd never actually been back east, Travis wondered how any part of New York could be described as homey. All that concrete and traffic noise and those buildings that jabbed at the sky like needles made him thankful he'd been born a country boy.

"This must be quite a change," he said as he hefted her bags from the bed of the truck. "Or have you been out west before?'' Perhaps she'd get homesick.

''No, I haven't traveled much.'' She didn't elaborate. ''Does anyone else live here with the two of you?'' she asked instead. ''I mean, in the house?''

''Nope.'' Baring his teeth in a grin, Travis headed for the back door. He opened it and stepped aside with a sweeping gesture. Who was he trying to impress, he wondered as she walked gingerly into the kitchen, as if she expected a ghost to pop out from behind the refrigerator. As if her feet still hurt.

''You need to get those boots off,'' he said gruffly as he shut the back door behind them. The kitchen was stuffy, the air stale. He opened a window in a vain attempt to catch a breeze. ''You bring any other shoes?''

Rory was so busy studying the huge kitchen that she almost missed his question. Her whole apartment could fit in here. There was a high ceiling, lots of cupboards with doors painted white and a six-burner stove. The floor was laid out in squares of black-and-white vinyl and the room was cleaner than she would have expected of two men, both apparently bachelors.

When she said as much, annoyance crossed Travis's face. ''Up until yesterday, we took all our meals down at the bunkhouse.''

She eyed him curiously. ''What happened yesterday?''

He leaned against the counter, worn denim pulled tight across the long muscles of his thighs. ''The ranch cook was called out of town.''

''The cook?'' she echoed. Of course a ranch would have a cook. The cowpunchers or cattle wranglers, or whatever they were called, had to eat, didn't they? "How long will he be gone?"

Travis took off his hat and studied it. "I don't know. His sister needed surgery. He went to be with her. But, like I said, we've got roundup to deal with. Extra ranch hands, extra work for everyone." He rotated the hat in his hands. "I've got to find a replacement, pronto." The last was muttered almost to himself.

"I could do it." The words popped from Rory's mouth without any conscious thought on her part.

He looked up with a smirk on his face. "Yeah? You have no idea what you'd be getting into."

His superior attitude goaded her like a cape flapping at a bull. "You need someone real bad?" she countered.

His chuckle was dry. "Not so bad I'd want the men to all quit the first day," he replied. "If the food ain't plain, hot and plentiful, they'll walk. I'll find someone if I have to bring in a caterer from somewhere, don't you worry."

Rory wandered around the kitchen, checking it out. Having something he wanted felt good. She turned and let her gaze wander over him boldly, almost insolently. He had the kind of rangy, powerful build men joined health clubs and sweated buckets to achieve, but she would bet he'd never worked out just to look good. His broad shoulders and lean torso had been sculpted by the same hard life that had weathered his skin and etched lines at the corners of his eyes. It was easy to see that Travis Winchester was no gentleman rancher.

"A caterer sounds expensive," she murmured, trailing her fingers over the worn tile of the counter.

He rolled his shoulders and set down his hat, brim up. "I'll find someone," he repeated, sounding annoyed.

From somewhere in the silent house, a clock chimed the hour. Between the two of them, something shifted subtly. Rory felt it, but she wasn't naive enough to think it was the balance of power. No, it was just the tug of awareness clicking up a notch. She could tell from his sudden tension that he felt it, too.

Did she really want to stay here in such close proximity to this man? He wasn't his brother—kind, easygoing Charlie.

Unreliable, irresponsible Charlie.

She hoped he came back soon to rescue her and that she was still here when he did.

"What's the job pay?" she asked.

It was Travis's turn to let his gaze sweep over her in obvious dismissal. "Forget it."

"Enough to cover my room and board?" she persisted, ignoring his tone.

He grinned and her breath caught. She filed away the image, and her reaction, for future contemplation.

"Yeah, but you won't be here that long," he said.

Rory shrugged. "I thought you were desperate, but if you aren't..." She let her voice trail off.

He rubbed his chin, eyeing her with an expression she couldn't quite interpret. "Oh, I'm desperate, all right."

She wondered if they were even discussing the same thing. There seemed to be another, silent conversation going on beneath the surface of the one they were having out loud.

"You don't happen to be some kind of fancy gourmet chef, do you?" he demanded, suddenly wary. "Charlie didn't say what kind of work you do, but my men won't eat food with unpronounceable names and ingredients they can't identify."

Casually, Rory held up one hand and studied her nails. "No, I'm not a fancy chef."

He snorted. "I didn't think so."

She stared full at him, unable to keep a slight grin from forming. "What I am, though, is a short-order cook. Plain, hot food and plenty of it."

His mocking smile faded as abruptly as the tan from a salon, but she couldn't resist another dig. "Now, are you willing to talk room and board while I'm waiting for Charlie, or do you still think a New York City hash slinger is too fancy to feed your crew?"

Chapter Three

While he did his best to digest Rory's startling announcement, Travis's mind whirled. Common sense clamored for him to take her up on her offer. His baser side agreed. Letting her stay at the house seemed like a logical plan, one with which only his survival instincts found fault.

The redhead was trouble, a city slicker. He knew that in his gut. She might as well have come with a capital *T* branded on her forehead.

"You can stay here," he said, not sure whether he was losing or winning his internal debate, "but only until I find another cook."

"Deal." She was smiling, her velvety lips curved upward at the corners. Faint freckles dusted her nose.

What was he getting himself into? "And no matter whether we've heard from Charlie by then or not," he clarified, watching her smile fade.

"We'll hear from him," she replied with a touch of the bravado he'd noticed before. "I know Charlie."

"I thought I did, too," Travis mumbled. For the first time, he wondered if Charlie, wherever he might be, was all right. Then he shrugged off the stab of concern. Charlie hadn't been abducted by aliens or hit his head and forgotten who he was. He'd left a note. The worst he might be was sunburned, broke or hung over, and Travis would have traded spots with him in a New York minute.

"Come on," he told Rory, "take off your boots so I can see how bad your feet are, and then I'll show you to your room. You must be tired."

Rory looked as if she was going to argue, but then she sat down in a kitchen chair and tugged off first one boot and then the other. In her stocking feet, she wiggled her toes experimentally and sighed with apparent relief.

"This feels so much better," she admitted. "But I can manage the rest on my own."

Squatting down beside her, Travis reached for one narrow foot. "A cook who can't stand up won't be much good to me," he said gruffly. "If you've got blisters, they need attention."

"If I have blisters, I'll let you know," she replied, scrambling to her feet.

He tipped back his head. From this perspective, her legs went on forever, he thought bemusedly. Then he, too, stood up. She was tall, but he could still stare her down. For a moment, neither gave an inch. Then he cleared his throat and turned away. "Let me know if you need some antiseptic cream. I'll show you to your room."

When they got to the top of the stairs, he led the way down the carpeted hall lined with doors. The pattern of colored glass in the round window at the end always reminded him of the cardboard kaleidoscopes he'd played with as a kid.

"That's Charlie's room," he said, pointing at the first door, which was closed. "I'm across the hall." He glanced inside. At least he'd made his bed this morning, but he'd left his socks on the floor. There was a pile of tack in one corner, a stack of books had fallen over, and his desk was covered with papers. Not that he cared what *she* thought, he just liked order.

He continued the tour. "The main bathroom's in there." He poked in his head, relieved to see it was reasonably clean. Charlie's razor and toothbrush were gone, another clue that he hadn't been forcibly removed.

"I've got my own bath, so we won't have to share." Travis pushed open a door at the end of the hall and went inside. So far, Rory hadn't said a word.

"Here's where you'll be staying." Travis ignored the spurt of dismay at the room's neglected appearance. Well, *he* hadn't known they were getting company.

Against one wall was a double bed, mattress bare. A small table made do as a nightstand, topped by a lamp with a water-spotted shade. A battered chest sat at the foot of the bed and a tall, scarred dresser faced it. The window had a plain pull-down shade, and the closet was empty except for a dozen wire hangers. A framed print of the Rocky Mountains, cut from a calendar, was the room's only decoration.

Several cardboard cartons were stacked in the corner, a cobweb floated from the ceiling light, and the walls needed paint. He was surprised Charlie hadn't done anything to make her feel more welcome.

If the same thought had occurred to Rory, she gave no sign. "This will be fine" was all she said.

Travis wondered how the room's appearance fitted with what she may have expected or been led to believe by his brother, but he could read nothing on her face. "I'll move those boxes out of here. There are sheets and towels in the hall closet." He gestured at the cedar chest. "Blankets in there, if you need them. I'll get your bags out of the truck."

"Thank you." Rory watched him disappear through the door. She didn't move until she heard his bootsteps on the staircase, and then she sat on the mattress with a tired sigh. This room was a far cry from what she had envisioned when she'd gotten Charlie's invitation, but so had been everything else since she'd stepped off the bus.

She glanced at the door, but there was no lock. Not that she considered Charlie's brother a threat—not one a locked door would keep out, anyway.

At least she had a place to stay. For a while, even that had seemed pretty uncertain. Now all she wanted to do was to lie down and sleep for twelve hours. Instead, she needed to get settled.

Suddenly she wondered if he expected her to fix an evening meal. And for how many?

By the time Travis returned with a suitcase in each hand, she was standing by the window, outwardly composed. He set them down on the chest at the end of the bed and then he crossed the hall to the bathroom.

Rory heard him rummaging around, and then he returned with a tube of antiseptic cream that he handed her.

Touched that he remembered, she thanked him.

"I have some chores I can't put off any longer," he said, making her feel guilty for having kept him from his work. "If there's anything else you need, I'll get it later. And don't worry about cooking tonight," he called over his shoulder. "Wes will fix something for the men. You and I can make do with sandwiches. I'll be back in a couple of hours."

Relief seeped through Rory. She would have enough time to unpack, check out the kitchen and maybe even take a shower. When she looked in the bathroom, she was pleased to see that, as well as the usual equipment, it had a modern tub-and-shower combination with a plastic curtain. A bottle of men's cologne, an aspirin bottle and a box of bandages were in the medicine cabinet over the sink, and one set of towels hung on the opposite wall, leaving plenty of room for her own supplies.

When Rory got back to the bedroom, she opened the window. The silence was a sound in itself. The breeze smelled faintly of grass and sunshine. Thinking of her tiny apartment back home with the endless traffic noises outside the window that was painted shut, the stale cooking smells in the hall and the cramped shower stall in the bathroom, she had to smile. Already, there was a lot to like in Colorado.

* * *

Travis caught up with his older brother Adam in one of the corrals where they kept the horses they rode daily. Adam had been out on the range with two of the regular cowhands and was just unsaddling his gelding. There were damp circles under the arms of his shirt and his leather chaps were dusty. Dirt and sweat streaked his face.

"What happened to you?" he demanded when he spotted Travis. "I didn't know you were taking the day off. There was a section of fence down in the far east pasture and it took us all morning just to round up the cows that went through it." He removed his Stetson and whacked it against his thigh. Dust rose in a fine cloud. "Could have used your help."

"I was busy." Technically, Adam was the boss, but they often worked independently.

Adam gave him a sharp look. "Was Charlie with you?" he asked. "He wasn't around today, either."

"No, Charlie wasn't with me," Travis replied.

"I hope you at least found a replacement for Flynn," Adam grumbled, referring to the cook. "If Wes fills in much longer, we'll have a mutiny on our hands."

Travis almost laughed out loud. "Well, I did that," he drawled. Then he began filling Adam in on his day, watching his brother's green eyes widen.

"Where the hell is Charlie now?" he demanded when Travis stopped for breath. "I can't believe he'd pull something like this."

"Then you didn't know anything about his writing to this woman, either?" Travis asked, perversely relieved to find out he'd been right. Charlie hadn't confided in Adam.

Adam shook his head. "The little sneak never breathed a word."

"That's not like Charlie, either," Travis mused. Usually, what Charlie knew, Charlie told. He wasn't big on keeping his own counsel. There had been times in high school when he was dating some girl Travis had the hots for and Travis had sincerely wished he would keep his mouth shut. Charlie had never revealed any really personal details, but Travis, usually dateless, hadn't appreciated his brother's innocent boasting.

"Where's Charlie's friend now?" Adam asked. "Has she already left for New York?"

"I hadn't gotten to that part," Travis admitted. "Actually, she's staying at the house for a few days."

Adam's black eyebrows rose. Of the three boys, he alone had their mother's coloring. Charlie's hair was brown, a couple of shades lighter than Travis's, and his eyes were brown, as well.

"She's staying with you?" Adam queried. "Is that wise? You don't know her, and Charlie's not here to explain."

Travis shoved his hands into the back pockets of his jeans and began to pace. "Hell, no, I don't think it's wise," he replied, voice rising on a note of pure frustration. So much for kidding himself that he was only keeping her here so she could cook. He hadn't even gotten to that part.

Adam was waiting patiently for some kind of explanation. He did that, just looked at you until you spilled your guts, even stuff you'd sworn you wouldn't tell him. Travis found himself wanting to scuff his toe in the dirt and stammer out his tumble of feelings. Instead, he tried to sound as if he had the situation well under control. Adam had enough on his mind.

"Turns out she's some kind of short-order cook in New York," he explained. "Nothing fancy, according to her. She wants to stay and wait for Charlie to come slinking back, so I told her she could keep the men fed for a few days until I find a real replacement for Flynn."

"You think she can handle it?" Adam asked.

Now Travis did grin. "I think she can handle whatever life throws at her."

Adam nodded, apparently satisfied, and went back to tending his horse. "Keep me posted" was all he said.

"How's Kim doing?" Travis asked. Kim was Adam's daughter, who was ten. A year before, his wife had announced she wasn't spending another winter on the ranch. She moved to Denver and got a divorce. Adam hadn't said much about it, except once to remark that the ranch lacked "excitement." Now Adam was raising Kim with the help of a full-time housekeeper.

He turned back to Travis with a grin that transformed him. "She's great," he said. "Right now she's mothering a litter of kittens and getting settled at school." He rolled his eyes. "She wants me to take her shopping for more clothes. At her age!"

Travis had to laugh. The idea of his brother picking out women's clothes, even for a ten-year-old, was pretty amusing.

"Maybe you can talk Mrs. Clark into going instead," he suggested.

Adam's smile faded. "I can't expect her to take the place of Kim's mother." Christie was working in an art gallery. The time she spent with her little girl could be recorded on the head of a horseshoe nail.

"I didn't mean—" Travis began.

Adam held up his hand. "I know you didn't. I guess where Kim's concerned I'm still trying to compensate." His voice grew quieter. "I can't help but wonder, if I'd spent more time with Christie—" He rubbed his hand over his face. "Doesn't matter now."

Sympathetic to his pain, Travis tried to think of something encouraging to say, but came up blank. "You'll work it out," he managed to say finally. "At least you have Kim."

"Yeah." Adam sighed and stretched his shoulders. "Let's hope Charlie comes home and straightens out this other mess. Any idea where he's gone?"

Travis shook his head. "And Rory is refusing to leave until she talks to him."

Adam's eyes narrowed. "Rory?" he echoed.

"Aurora Mancini." Travis nearly suggested Adam come by and meet her, and then something held him back.

"I'll be by your place to check her out," Adam said, "but I suppose I'll let her settle in first. You want Mrs. Clark to fix you two something for supper?"

"No, thanks. I figured we could make do with sandwiches tonight. I'll give her a quick tour of the bunkhouse kitchen, and then, in the morning, she can go to work."

"Good deal. Maybe, if she does a halfway decent job, the men won't quit, after all." Adam removed his mount's bridle and gave him a slap on the rump. The big bay ambled toward the group of horses in the far corner of the corral. "I hope you know what you're doing," he added before he ducked beneath the bars of the fence and headed for the feed bin in the barn.

"So do I," Travis muttered under his breath. "So do I."

Rory was setting the kitchen table when she heard Travis on the back porch. She'd found ham, fresh bread and sandwich makings, plus some chilled canned pears. For dessert there was always ice cream from the freezer, which she had been relieved to see was well stocked.

When he came in, hanging his hat on a hook by the door and raking a hand through his hair, he glanced at the answering machine on the counter.

"Anyone call?"

Rory wondered if he was thinking about Charlie. "No. The phone didn't ring. Supper's ready whenever you are," she said. "I took you literally and made ham sandwiches. I hope that's okay."

"Sounds great. I'll wash up and be right back down."

While he was gone, she poured iced tea. A relaxing shower and a change of clothes had revived her. In deference to the heat, most of her hair was piled on top of her head and held with a plastic clip embedded with glitter. With her neck bared to the air stirred by the overhead fan, she felt almost human again. Her natural optimism had returned. Charlie would show up with a logical explanation, she and Travis would become friends, and the money she had lost would be restored to her.

Well, she'd settle for two out of three.

Travis had washed off the worst of the dust, combed his hair and was headed back to the kitchen when he heard Rory's humming. Listening to the clear, sweet notes, he hesitated in midstep.

After one glimpse of her in purple shorts and a top that left her trim waist bare, he'd fled up the stairs like a rabbit with a coyote on its tail. Her image was still permanently etched onto his brain. She had the long legs, tiny waist and rounded breasts of the teen dolls his niece collected.

The problem was that Rory was flesh and blood, not plastic, and she was going to be sleeping under his roof. Travis glanced at the ceiling, gritting his teeth, and wondered if Charlie had any idea how miserable he was making his brother's life.

Rory was standing by the counter fiddling with the sandwiches when he showed up, determined to keep his expression blank and his tongue from hanging out. The wall phone next to her rang and she jumped. Apparently Travis wasn't the only one feeling the tension between them.

"I'll get that." Carefully, he reached past her, trying not to inhale her perfume, and lifted the receiver.

He wasn't even thinking about Charlie until the familiar voice greeted him.

"Hi, bro. Did Rory arrive safely?"

Travis's grip tightened on the receiver as his gaze darted to where she stood in the middle of the room. "Where the hell are you?" he demanded.

Rory tensed and her face went pale.

"Just wanted you to know I'm okay," Charlie replied, ignoring the question. "Is she there? How's she settling in?"

"How do you know she stayed?" Travis asked.

"She did, didn't she?" Charlie's voice went up a notch.

"Why don't you ask her?" If Charlie was so concerned about his bride-to-be, why hadn't he stuck around?

"No, wait!" he exclaimed before Travis could hand the receiver to Rory. "I can't talk to her now. I'll hang up, I swear."

Rory was reaching for the phone. "Let me talk to him."

Afraid Charlie would make good his threat, Travis shook his head and turned partly away from her. "Where are you?" he repeated. "What in Hades is going on?"

"Never mind that," Charlie replied maddeningly. "Just tell me, is Rory going to stay at the house?"

"What?" Travis lowered his voice slightly, but he knew she could still hear every word. "What else was I supposed to do? She won't leave until she talks to you. When are you coming back?"

"Soon," Charlie replied. "Just don't let her go, okay?" For a moment there was the sound of static and then a sharp click as the line went dead.

"Charlie!" Travis shouted into the receiver, even though he knew it was futile. "Charlie, answer me!" The phone remained silent. "Oh, for—" Frustrated, he slammed down the receiver and glared at Rory.

"Was that Charlie? What did he say?" she demanded, grabbing it and pressing it to her ear.

"Charlie? Charlie, where are you?" She hung up when she heard a dial tone. Color had flooded her pale cheeks and her blue eyes were shooting sparks. The silly plastic doohickey perched on her head wobbled precariously as strands of hair escaped it to curl around her neck and ears like licks of flame. "Why did you let him hang up?" she wailed. "Where is he? What's going on?"

"I didn't let him. I think we were cut off," Travis said through gritted teeth. "He asked about you, and before I could find out anything, the line went dead."

She planted her hands on her hips and eyed him suspiciously. "That's it? That's all he said?"

"That's it," Travis echoed. Maybe Charlie would call back.

"He might have told me where he is." Her tone was accusing. Did she think he was trying to keep her and Charlie apart?

"Charlie threatened to hang up if I gave the phone to you." Realizing he was shouting, Travis ran a hand over his face. When he looked again, Rory's eyes had filled with tears. Oh, hell, he hated to see a woman cry.

He thought about trying to comfort her and wondered where he could safely put his hands. "Don't cry," he said instead.

Her tears only fell faster. Now what was he supposed to do? He almost felt like crying himself.

"Maybe Charlie misunderstood," he hedged. "Maybe *I* misunderstood." He hadn't, but the tiny fib seemed to placate her. She sniffled and looked up through eyes that reminded him of violets after a spring storm, drenched and vulnerable. With a groan, he damned the consequences and pulled her into his arms.

Rory stiffened as his cheek, rough with whiskers, scraped hers. He smelled of soap and leather. The hands she'd flung out were pressed against his shoulders; their knees bumped awkwardly. As she struggled against the tears, and against him, the sounds he was making began to penetrate.

Wordless sounds. Soothing, shushing noises one would use on a frightened child or a skittish horse. His arms closed around her in a protective circle. Comforting, undemanding. Rory allowed herself to go limp, to slide her hands down his chest and around his waist. He was rock solid. She sighed and snuggled closer to his warmth.

Mmm. It felt so good to be held.

Briefly, his arms tightened. Then, to her disappointment, he pulled away.

Bemused, she released her grip on his shirt and smiled up at him, her vision still blurry from her tears.

"Sorry." His voice was thick and his cheeks were flaming.

Rory blinked and her vision cleared. He stared at some point past her shoulder, his face set in grim lines.

Reality was like a plunge into icy water. "That's okay." She searched for something to say that would dispel the sudden awkwardness between them, but neither her tongue nor her brain seemed to be working right. Both felt slow and clumsy. Giving up on the witty, reassuring comment that wouldn't come, she turned instead to food as a distraction. "Are you hungry?" she managed to ask.

Relief flickered across his stoic countenance. ‘‘Starved.’’

‘‘It’s just sandwiches,’’ she reminded him.

His head bobbed and he met her gaze. ‘‘Sandwiches will be great, just great.’’ His tone was falsely hearty, his smile strained, his movements jerky as he pulled out a chair. Then he hesitated.

‘‘Sit,’’ she ordered, frustrated by the awkwardness between them. Glory be. He’d only been comforting her.

He sat down as if his legs had been shot out from under him. Rory set a plate of sandwiches in front of him. She gave him a glass of iced tea as he watched her warily.

‘‘Eat.’’ She dropped into a chair across from him. When he continued to stare, food untouched, she frowned at the table in sudden concern. Had she made some mistake in fixing the meal? ‘‘What’s wrong?’’

‘‘I’m sorry about Charlie,’’ Travis said quietly. ‘‘This must be difficult for you.’’

His words caught her totally off guard. New tears flooded her eyes and she dashed them away with her fingers, embarrassed. She’d been through worse than this and never cried once!

She ducked her head. ‘‘Thanks. I know you’re worried, too.’’

‘‘Yeah, but at least now I know he’s alive.’’ His voice was soft, but when she gave him a watery smile and he saw her tears, he came half out of his chair. ‘‘Oh, Lord, don’t start that again.’’

The panic in his voice lightened her mood. ‘‘I’m okay,’’ she told him with a lingering smile. ‘‘Really. It’s just been a very long day.’’

For a moment he studied her as if he were looking for signs of another outburst. Then he nodded, apparently satisfied, and reached for a sandwich. For a few moments, they both ate silently. Rory was surprised at her appetite. Travis ate his way through two thick sandwiches and a bowl of canned pears.

"That was good," he said as he drained the rest of his iced tea. "Did you make any coffee?" He glanced around the kitchen as Rory popped to her feet.

"No, but I can."

He seemed to hesitate. "Thanks," he said after a moment. "That would be nice. Did you find the coffeemaker?"

"Yes. I'll just be a minute."

While he watched her measure the grounds and pour the water, he sat back in his chair and munched idly on a carrot stick. He felt bad, knowing she must be tired, but waiting on her now would only complicate the issue. Holding her the way he had made things awkward. His body's reaction to her nearness had certainly clouded things for him!

He only hoped she hadn't felt his response.

Charlie hadn't called back, Travis realized as he watched her take a mug from the cupboard. Wait till Travis caught up with him.

"Did you find sheets and stuff?" he asked.

"Yes, thanks."

After that moment when she'd been plastered against his chest, the sudden formality of her tone now seemed doubly out of place. Maybe she, too, was trying to regain her footing, or perhaps she *had* felt him and been repulsed by his very physical reaction.

Already he missed the sensation of having her gathered against him, a complication he sure as heck didn't need.

"How do you take it?" she asked crisply.

Travis looked at her blankly, and then he noticed the full mug in her hand. "Black."

While she hovered, he took a sip and thanked her. Then he marshalled his thoughts and focused on the matter at hand. If she was to start cooking in the morning, they had a few things to go over.

"Mighty good, ma'am," one of the cowhands told Rory politely as he came back for a healthy second helping of ham, fried potatoes, pancakes and eggs.

She beamed at the little man the others called Gus, relieved that her first efforts seemed to be appreciated. The stove in the bunkhouse kitchen was a massive commercial model with eight burners and a griddle. Luckily for Rory, the regular cook had left the kitchen well stocked and the freezer full.

Flipping more pancakes onto a waiting plate, she checked the bowls of peaches and blueberries and then glanced over to where Travis sat at a long table with the men. Except for a nod and a quick inspection of the food she'd prepared when he first came in, he had ignored her. The evening before, he'd given her a quick tour of the facility and a list of instructions she'd struggled to retain. Still, except for the quantity and allowing for regional favorites, slinging hash was pretty much the same in one place as another.

There was a dog-eared cookbook filled with handwritten notes under the counter. Rory planned to study it the first moment she got. She wanted to do a good job. Even when Charlie got back, she would need something to do. She had no idea how long the roundup would last, but men always needed to eat.

Besides, thanks to a cruel twist of fate and a lapse in judgment on her part, her options had narrowed to one, and that one had disappeared. It was time to make her own options, and this was a chance she didn't intend blowing.

"This is my brother, Adam," Travis said from right in front of Rory, startling her so badly that she nearly dropped the spatula she'd been holding. Beside him stood an equally tall, equally weather- and work-honed man with shaggy black hair. A little girl was holding his hand. Despite the differences in the two men's coloring, Rory could see a family resemblance between them. Although Adam was dressed in rugged work clothes like Travis and the rest of the men, there was something about his expression and the way he held himself that set him apart. Where Travis seemed to bristle with energy, even impatience, Adam appeared more reserved, almost resigned. He was studying Rory with a polite smile that didn't quite reach his green eyes as he extended his hand.

"Nice to meet you," he said quietly. "Thanks for helping us out with the cooking."

Rory resisted the urge to pat down her hair and check her blouse for spills; instead, she slipped her hand briefly into his. Although his perusal made her a little nervous, it wasn't the same breathless kind of feeling she got when Travis glanced in her direction. Odd, Adam was conventionally more attractive. In comparison, with his full mustache and the stubble he hadn't bothered to shave off this morning, Travis looked like a saddle tramp.

Seeing the two Winchester brothers side by side, Rory wondered which of them Charlie resembled more.

"This is my daughter Kim," Adam said, resting his hand on the child's shoulder. She had green eyes like his and dark brown hair.

Rory stuck out her hand. "Hi, sweetie. I'm Rory Mancini."

Kim shook it gravely, her expression intense. "You're from New York." She made it sound as though Rory had come from Mars.

Rory smothered a chuckle. "Yes, I am."

"What's it like?" Kim asked.

"Big, crowded," Rory replied. "Not like here, that's for sure."

Adam stroked his hand down Kim's long hair. "You'll have to talk to Rory later, honey. She's fixing breakfast for the men."

"I'll look forward to it," Rory told her, hoping she wasn't overstepping the bounds. After all, right now she was more employee than guest.

"Me, too." Kim's smile, though shy, was very sweet.

"Is there anything special I can fix for you?" Rory asked them.

"Thanks, but we ate at the house," Adam replied.

"Mrs. Clark fixed French toast," Kim added. "I had three pieces."

Adam glanced at his watch before Rory could say anything else. "We'd better get you out to the bus stop," he told Kim. After they both said goodbye to Rory, Travis asked Adam if he'd called the vet. They walked away with Kim between them. Rory was admiring the picture the three of them made when Kim turned back and waved. As soon as she and her dad went out the door, the other men began shoving back their chairs and getting to their feet. A couple of them smiled and waved at Rory before leaving. Travis wasn't one of them.

As the men's voices receded, she looked at the dirty dishes scattered across the length of the table and then at the stove. With lunches to pack, she had her work cut out for her before they came back looking for another meal.

While she was tackling the mess, Travis and Adam were in the process of saddling up.

"She's not what I expected," Adam said over his mount's broad back. "And not what I would have guessed Charlie would pick."

"That's for sure." Travis tightened the cinch on his buckskin. He'd been impressed with the meal she had served up this morning, as competently as if she'd been doing it for years. Perhaps she had. He realized how little he knew about her and her life. "Our brother seems to be full of surprises these days."

Adam was using a hoof-pick on his bay's hind foot. "Sure you don't mind putting her up at your place?" he asked. "She could be a real distraction."

Travis's head snapped up. "What do you mean?"

"Just that you're not used to having a houseguest," Adam replied mildly. "Especially a woman. What did you think I meant?"

While Adam waited, obviously puzzled by Travis's defensive tone, Travis suddenly got busy rechecking the cinch on his horse's saddle.

"What did you think I meant?" Adam repeated.

"Nothing. Why?" Travis turned around one of Adam's own tricks, answering a question with another question.

Now Adam merely shrugged. "No reason, I guess. I just wish Charlie would get his sorry butt back here. We need him."

"We can cover for him if we have to. Did you call the stock hauler?" Travis leaped on the change of subject, relieved to be out from under his elder brother's scrutiny.

"Yeah. The trucks will be here next week. All we have to do is have the cows ready to load." Adam glanced at his watch. "I've got to stop at the barn on the way out. I promised Kim I'd vaccinate that litter of kittens she's been mothering."

"Go ahead. I'll catch you later," Travis responded. "I want to change Butch's bridle. He doesn't seem to like this bit." It wasn't that he wanted to be rid of Adam; he was just too tired to guard his mouth. Any more slipups where Rory was concerned and Adam would be on him like a cow dog on a runaway heifer.

Travis busied himself with adjusting the bridle and finding a spare pair of gloves. Finally he mounted up. As he rode out, he looked in the direction of the bunkhouse, but the kitchen was on the other side of the long, low building. He thought about checking on Rory, but he stifled the urge. She was a New York City short-order cook, he reminded himself. No doubt she was coping just fine.

Chapter Four

"Where are you from?" asked Jane, the woman who had appeared at the bunkhouse kitchen after breakfast to help Rory with the cleanup. Married to one of the ranch hands, she was a little woman with light blond hair and a wiry build. Next to her compact efficiency, Rory felt all gangly arms and legs.

While Rory had thrown together sandwiches and packed lunches earlier, Jane loaded the dishwasher and cleaned up the kitchen area. Now she was wiping off the long table where the men had eaten breakfast.

"I'm from New York," Rory replied, wondering just how much of her situation to disclose.

"I've never been there," Jane said, "but I went to Chicago once for a funeral, and of course we go into Denver a lot. Barney doesn't like to fly, so we always drive." She straightened a couple of chairs. "You see a lot that way, so I don't really mind. I don't think I'd like the pollution or the crime in New York. Or commuting to work. My commute takes five minutes. Guess I'm just a homebody at heart.''

Rory refrained from pointing out there were elements in any big city most people didn't like. There were trade-offs, like anywhere else. Like Colorado.

Jane had already mentioned that home was a small house on Winchester land where she and Barney had lived for ten years with their kids, who were grown now. Rory wished she could ask Jane about Charlie, but the opportunity didn't present itself and she didn't want to appear obvious. When the two women had finished with their work, they left the sack lunches for someone to pick up and walked out of the bunkhouse together.

In the bright sunshine, Jane stopped and looked around, clearly perplexed. An old green truck was parked by itself. ''Where's your car?'' she asked.

''I don't have one.'' In New York, Rory had ridden public transportation. She wondered what the other woman would think if she confessed that, although she possessed a drivers' license, she had never owned a vehicle.

Reaching into the purse slung over her arm, Jane pulled out a lighter and a pack of cigarettes. She offered one to Rory, who declined, and then she lit one and stuck it into her mouth. Eyes narrowed against the acrid smoke, she inhaled deeply and coughed. ''I needed that,'' she rasped. ''How'd you get here? Did someone drop you off?''

Rory's situation wasn't going to remain a secret

forever. "I'm staying at Travis's," she admitted, prepared for a barrage of questions.

Jane looked only faintly surprised. "Well, I don't suppose you'd want to sleep at the bunkhouse with the men," she said philosophically. "Most of 'em snore. Can I give you a lift?"

Rory was relieved to be let off the hook so easily. She didn't ask how Jane knew so many of the men snored. "No, thanks. I can walk." It would feel good to get the kinks out, and she could see the house from where they stood.

Jane shrugged. "Okay. At least it's cooler today. Weather changes like a teenager changes clothes. I'll see you back here later."

Rory began walking as Jane climbed into the truck and drove off in the other direction. The first thing Rory did when she got to the house was to check the answering machine for messages, but the light stared back at her like an unblinking red eye.

She opened the fridge and grabbed a cold soda, glanced at the round clock over the sink and wandered into the large living room. She had been too tired to pay much attention to her surroundings the day before. The furniture here was all oversize, massive pieces of dark wood upholstered in gloomy colors. Somehow, despite the similarities in tone and texture, none of the pieces actually went together.

Over the stone fireplace an elk head with cobwebs on its antlers contrasted with the high-tech appearance of the big-screen television in one corner. Magazines covered a table next to a brown leather chair. The top one sported a photo of a well-endowed bull. The wood floor had once been stained a deep walnut, but the finish was scratched and worn around the edges of an oval rug whose colors had been dulled with time.

The room didn't invite Rory to sit down; it was too masculine. Although Travis had told her he'd grown up here, the house bore no woman's mark. Rory wondered why not.

After taking a long swallow of her soda and letting its chilled sweetness run down her dry throat, she headed upstairs to her room. Her feet ached; her back and shoulders were sore. Feeding over a half-dozen hearty appetites at once was different from feeding ten in a row, she realized, and she still had supper to deal with.

When she got to the top of the stairs, she saw that Travis's bedroom door was open. She was alone in the house, but she still glanced nervously over her shoulder before succumbing to temptation and peeking inside.

His room was nearly as sparsely furnished as her own, his only apparent concessions to comfort a king-size bed and a bentwood rocker with a frayed cane seat. The tick of an old-fashioned windup clock poked at the silence. In one corner was a pile of bridles. Next to the rocking chair sat a tall lamp. On the floor was a stack of books. Curious, Rory set her soda can on the dresser and squatted down to look closer.

The top book was a tome on range management, which didn't surprise her. What did was that the book beneath it was a paperback thriller she'd finished on the plane. Under that was a collection of short stories by Southern writers. On the bottom of the pile was the biography of a former president.

From downstairs, the grandfather clock chimed the hour. Feeling as guilty as if she'd been snooping through Travis's underwear drawer, Rory replaced his books exactly as she had found them and tiptoed from the room. She didn't realize until she was at the end of the hall that she had passed Charlie's closed door without a bit of curiosity. Setting her travel alarm for an hour's nap, she collapsed onto her bed and closed her eyes.

"Here come the locusts," Jane joked later that afternoon as she set bottles of ketchup and jars of salsa on the long table in the bunkhouse kitchen. Through the open windows came the sounds of men's voices and the tramp of their boots.

Feeling her stomach tighten with nerves, Rory tried to pick out Travis's deep voice from the rest, but couldn't. Had he heard from Charlie yet? How did Travis feel about the disappearance of the man she claimed she was going to marry? She was embarrassed that he might think Charlie had needed to escape her.

How long could she hang around and wait for him? Her funds were limited and she'd need to find a real job if he didn't show up soon.

The first of the men trouped through the door and headed down the hall to clean up before they ate. For the next few minutes, Rory was distracted from watching for Travis as she filled serving dishes and platters with thick slices of roast beef, boiled potatoes, macaroni and cheese, applesauce and green beans seasoned with bacon. In moments, the men came back and sat down, their clothes stained and dusty, their freshly washed faces etched with fatigue.

Looking as dirty and tired as the rest of them, Travis finally appeared on his way to wash up. Rory caught his eye and he nodded, his somber expression unchanging. By the time he came back, she'd managed to burn her thumb on the pan of rolls and slop gravy down the front of her apron. No doubt her hair was poking out around the bandanna she'd tied over it, and her face was probably shiny with perspiration. The lip gloss she'd dashed on during one of Jane's smoke breaks earlier in the afternoon was long gone.

A couple of the other men greeted Rory by name as she hurried back and forth between the table and the stove, carrying steaming bowls of food.

"What's for supper?" Gus called out.

"Snakes and snails," she replied.

"Hey, Wes," a heavyset man named Sam drawled, "she fixed one of your recipes."

Wes was the man who'd been filling in since the regular cook left. This morning he had taken a minute to ask if she had any questions before he headed out with the others. Now his dark eyes met hers. "Probably tastes better," he said with a grin.

Rory smiled back. These men weren't unlike her regular customers at the diner. They just dressed differently.

Before she could head Travis off and ask about Charlie, he sat down at one end of the table with the men and was immediately drawn into a discussion. Chewing her lip in frustration, Rory set down the platter of roast beef at his elbow. The wrangler sitting across from him began helping himself, but Travis never looked up. Spinning on her heel, Rory headed back to the stove to get another bowl of food.

A couple of gallon milk containers were making the rounds, and Jane was pouring coffee. As soon as everyone else was served, Rory and Jane filled their own plates. Jane sat down at the opposite end of the table from Travis, next to her husband. Barney was a skinny fellow with a beard and friendly blue eyes. Rory sat across from them. For the next ten minutes, there was relative silence as everyone concentrated on their heaping plates.

Rory took the opportunity to sneak a few looks at Travis. He was wearing a leather vest over a red plaid shirt and he'd removed his hat. His damp hair, freshly combed back from his forehead, was beginning to wave as it dried. A lock had fallen forward and he brushed it back absently. His hands, she noticed, were long and narrow. The backs were tanned and the nails were neatly clipped.

"Hey, boss, how do things look in that east section?" asked Gus.

As he replied in his deep, measured voice, it sounded to Rory as if they knew each individual cow. Quickly, she cleaned her plate and took her dishes to the sink. She would have liked to listen. Instead, she replenished serving bowls and watched with horror as the men dished up second helpings as large as the first. The huge amounts of food she'd fixed disappeared with alarming speed. Just when it looked as if she was going to run out of everything, a man whose name she had forgotten leaned back, set down his fork and patted his barrel of a stomach. He belched softly behind his hand.

"Got any dessert?" he asked her. He had a gray ponytail and several missing teeth.

"You betcha." Several more of the men watched her with an interest she suspected had far less to do with her personally than it did with the peach cobbler she'd baked earlier. As fast as she dished it up, Jane cleared away the dirty dishes and replaced them with the cobbler. Amid the rumble of pleased comments, Rory grabbed a tub of ice cream from the freezer and a scoop from the utensil drawer.

"You married?" asked a young man who looked as if he was still in his teens as she worked her way around the table, plopping a scoop of ice cream on each plate Jane set down.

Rory remembered his name from breakfast. She returned his bold grin with a smile of her own. "No, Steve. You asking?"

He blushed bright red amid a chorus of derisive hoots.

"If you keep feeding us like this, I may just have to propose," he muttered around a mouthful of the cobbler. Then he twisted away as Sam, sitting next to him, poked out his elbow.

"Bet she kisses as good as she cooks." Sam's flat face bore a speculative expression as he stared at Rory. His grin held no warmth.

Suppressing a shudder, Rory ignored him. Back in the Bronx, she'd certainly heard worse comments. Her ex-husband, the manager at the diner where she worked, had never wanted to alienate a customer, so she'd gotten used to turning a deaf ear.

"Anyone else want ice cream?" She glanced around the table until her attention rested on Travis's bent head. As if he could feel her gaze, he raised eyes an unreadable as smoke. He glanced at the ice cream and Rory plopped some on his plate. His quiet thanks was nearly drowned out by a shout of laughter from the other end of the table.

Had he thought she was too friendly with the men? Too flirtatious with Steve? He certainly hadn't given her any indication that he approved of her relationship with Charlie. The plain truth was that he didn't want her here, that was all. She could cook a gourmet feast or greasy hash and it wouldn't alter a thing. Travis just didn't like her and she wasn't going to change that. From what he'd said before about fancy food, he'd probably prefer the hash.

Rory hesitated, but this wasn't the time or place to inquire about Charlie. She had no idea what the others had been told about his sudden absence—or her equally sudden appearance. They seemed to accept her presence as the new cook; but what would they think when word of where she was staying got around?

When she had finished serving everyone, she crossed the kitchen to put away the rest of the ice cream. Jane was loading the stack of dinner plates into the dishwasher. On the range and the counter teetered a mountain of dirty dishes and utensils.

"The peach cobbler was a big hit," Jane said as she put a handful of silverware into the utility basket. "There isn't a speck of it left."

"I used one of the regular cook's recipes," Rory replied as she poked through the big refrigerator, mentally planning the next day's menu. "Thank goodness he left his book behind. I'm not used to cooking for this kind of crowd.''

Jane glanced up. ''You aren't? Where'd you work before?''

Rory was about to reply when Travis spoke from behind her.

''Make up a grocery list,'' he said. ''Let me know when you need supplies. Jane will run you into town and you can put them on the ranch account.''

Rory nearly dropped the carton of eggs she was holding. What was wrong with her?

It was obvious that he was waiting for her to say something. ''Okay,'' she managed to squeak, nerves jangling from his sudden closeness.

''We'll have four extra men starting in the morning. They're here for the roundup,'' he added over his shoulder as he walked away.

''Wonderful,'' Rory murmured, but he didn't act as though he heard her.

''He's never been married,'' Jane volunteered, staring after him as he left the kitchen. ''I don't recall that he's even gotten close. Waste of a good man, if you ask me.''

Rory wasn't sure how to respond. It was Charlie she wanted to talk about, not Travis. ''Maybe he's just never met the right woman,'' she said lamely.

''Maybe not. Do you think he's handsome?'' Jane filled the sink with hot water as Rory scraped out pots and pans. There were no leftovers, but she'd cooked an extra roast for the next day's sandwiches.

She set the large chunk of meat on a cutting board and started slicing. ''Travis?'' she asked, although she knew darn well who Jane meant. ''Uh, sure. He's okay.'' That seemed like a safe enough answer. Any woman with eyes in her head would have to admit he had a certain rugged appeal. Throw in that loose-limbed, lord-of-all-he-surveyed saunter and the husky voice…

Rory realized she was staring into space with a bemused grin on her face, remembering how it had felt to be held in his arms the evening before. She straightened abruptly, amazed she hadn't cut herself with the big knife. Heat climbed her cheeks.

''If you like the type,'' she added with a frown of concentration. If she remembered right, Charlie had mentioned in one of his letters that Travis was in his early thirties and single. Now that she thought about it, Charlie had mentioned his brother frequently. Perhaps Travis was a confirmed bachelor. So what did he do during the long Colorado winters, watch television? That certainly accounted for that monstrosity of a set she'd noticed at the house.

''What's not to like about him?'' Jane demanded. ''Tall, honest, handsome and successful.'' She ticked off each quality on a soapy finger as water dripped on the floor. ''Can you tell me why the man's still single?''

Rory assumed she was supposed to answer. ''Because Colorado women are shy?'' she guessed with a weak smile, earning a snort of disgust from her companion. Granted, Travis wasn't the most garrulous man around, but that wouldn't even slow down some of the single females she knew back home. They'd swarm all over him. She was surprised how much the idea irritated her.

Jane turned and plunged her hands back into the

sink. "I guess running this big ranch has kept him too busy to go out and find someone." After a pause, she added, "But sometimes you don't have to go out looking for love. It comes right after you."

Rory stared at Jane's back with a sinking feeling of dismay. What was going through her mind?

"How did you meet Barney?" she asked, in a desperate bid to change the subject. She didn't want to hear any more about Travis. It was Charlie she should be curious about. Too late, she realized she could have asked Jane about *him,* but the other woman had already launched into the tale of meeting her husband on a hayride.

When Travis got back to the house that evening, the first thing he did was to breathe a sigh of relief that Rory was nowhere in sight, and the second was to check the answering machine for messages. Damn Charlie, anyway. What kind of game was he playing?

Travis had made the mistake of stopping by Adam's house for some papers on his way back here an hour ago and had been roped into going over the next day's schedule for the umpteenth time. Adam was obsessive when it came to detail, and he wanted the calves rounded up before prices dropped. Then Kim had asked Travis to help with her math homework. Feeling guilty for neglecting her lately, he hadn't wanted to say no.

Whenever he ventured through Adam's back door into the large, modern kitchen, he remembered how Christie had insisted that everyone except "employees," as she called the wranglers, use the front entry.

From the time Adam first brought her home from

college as his bride, Travis could feel the tension between them. Despite the new house Adam had built her, she'd never gotten used to the ranch and she hated Colorado winters. It hadn't been that big a surprise when she finally hightailed it back to civilization, leaving behind a stunned husband and a brokenhearted child. After all, their mother had done the same thing—except that she'd left three children behind instead of just one.

Never mind the past. This had been a long day, made longer by Adam. Travis hadn't slept all that well last night, but it wasn't the roundup that had kept him awake. Despite his brother's obsessing, Travis figured the roundup would come off the same as usual—more dependent on the calf crop, luck and the market than on anything they did to control the outcome. About the only thing Travis felt in control of right now was the water temperature in the shower he was looking forward to taking before he fell, face forward, into bed.

He listened for sounds from Rory's room, but he didn't hear anything except the normal grunts and groans of an old house settling for the night. After the day she'd put in, she'd probably turned in early. It wasn't as if she would have wanted to stay up to hear about the fence he'd repaired or the cows he'd doctored. They had nothing in common except Charlie.

Without bothering to turn on the television, Travis sat down in the leather chair that had belonged to his father and pulled off his boots. Leaving them in the living room, he tiptoed up the steps in his socks.

As he reached the top of the stairs, Rory's door

flew open and out she tumbled wearing a skimpy little set of pajamas that bared legs nearly as long as a Thoroughbred's but a whole lot prettier. Her outfit was made of some silky material in the same bright pink as a severe sunburn and nearly as clinging. Travis could only stare, fascinated, like a kid with his first girlie magazine.

When Rory saw the big bulk of his form in the dimness, she nearly screamed before she realized who it was.

"What are you doing, lurking around like a burglar?" she demanded, one hand pressed to her wildly beating heart as she collapsed against the door of her room. She'd still been half-asleep as she'd stumbled from bed, but now she was wide-awake. "You scared the heck out of me."

Whiskers blurred the line of Travis's jaw, and his eyes were shadowed with weariness. He'd removed his hat and boots, but he was still big. Since Rory was barefoot, he topped her by several inches.

"I thought you were asleep," he said defensively. "I was trying to be quiet."

He was being considerate, and she'd accused him of sneaking around in his own house. "I'm sorry," she said. "I just woke up."

Travis's gaze wandered over her and his lips twitched. Belatedly remembering how little her pajamas covered, Rory ducked behind her bedroom door and peered at him around the edge. Her robe was in storage, and now the glass of water she'd been after had lost its appeal.

"I didn't mean to startle you," Travis replied. "I should have left on my boots and stamped my feet."

"Don't change your normal habits for me," Rory told him hastily. "I don't want to inconvenience you any more than I already have."

His eyes narrowed. "You mean I can walk around in the buff like I usually do?" he asked, straight-faced. "Charlie and I don't stand on ceremony around here."

She wasn't sure how to respond. Was he teasing her? "Uh, that would be fine, as long as you warned me, I guess." She tried to ignore the image that flew into her head. Funny, she had never imagined Charlie naked. That must be because she hadn't actually met him yet. Maybe Travis had a photo of him somewhere. She hadn't realized until now that there didn't seem to be any family pictures in the house.

"You wouldn't mind?" Travis was clearly surprised by her comment that she didn't care if he went naked.

Oh, dear.

As heat washed over her, she blinked away the mental image of him and prayed he had no idea what she'd been thinking. If he remembered comforting her the night before, he gave no sign. "Have you heard anything?" she asked.

Her query about Charlie brought Travis back to reality with a crash and reminded him why she was here. Not to add substance to his own solitary dreams, that was for sure. "I've been at Adam's house, and he didn't call there," he told her. "Maybe tomorrow."

"Yeah." Her smile trembled and her hair glowed in the lamplight like banked coals. "You must be tired. I won't keep you any longer," she apologized, fluffing her curls with one hand. "Just ignore me, okay?"

Ignore her—in that outfit? As if he could. She must have him mixed up with one of the steers they were sending to market next week. From the way he kept reacting to her, he felt more like a randy bull that had been penned up way too long.

Not the way a man wanted to react to his brother's intended. Travis was about to excuse himself when she shifted and the scooped neck of her pajama top slid off her shoulder. Her skin was as unmarked as a fresh snowfall, her bones surprisingly delicate for such a tall woman. With painful clarity, he remembered how fragile she had felt in his arms.

Her eyes, when he forced himself to look up, were the dark, clear blue of a mountain lake, and her mouth—with its pouty bow and full lower lip—was going to keep him awake all night. His imagination taunted him further by showing him an image of her sprawled across his bed in that same ridiculous outfit. And then without it.

Hell's bells, what kind of a man was he? She belonged to Charlie—at least until Charlie told him otherwise.

The reminder didn't help.

"Don't you have a robe?" he demanded as the results of a long, restless night and a stressful day began hammering at his temples.

She colored, her face nearly matching the pink of her outfit, and she retreated farther behind the barrier of the door. "It took up too much room in the suitcase."

Damn, now he'd made her feel as awkward as he

did. He thought of offering her Charlie's bathrobe, but something in him rebelled at the image of her wearing it so close to all that skin. "Just a minute." He ducked back into his room and came out with a dark green velvet robe Adam and Christie had given him for Christmas one year. He'd never worn it.

"Here." He thrust the garment at Rory. "Use this."

She had to come out from behind the door to take it. "I can't possibly. It looks brand-new." She held it up like a shield, its rich, mossy darkness making her skin appear nearly translucent in contrast.

When she tried to give it back, Travis shoved his hands behind him. "Keep it," he said, resisting the urge to stroke that creamy shoulder with the tips of his fingers. "It would never look that good on me."

She hesitated, and then she smiled. "Well, maybe I will just borrow it." She started to retreat into her room.

Despite his fatigue and his agitation, Travis wanted to keep her in the hall for a moment longer. He had the good sense of a cow on loco weed.

"You did fine today," he said when she would have shut her door in his face. "Did you have any problems?"

The crack in the door widened, and her full lips curved into a smile. "Not really. Jane was a lifesaver." Her expression grew anxious. "I thought we were going to run out of food at supper. Were there any complaints?"

He nearly laughed out loud, remembering how the men had raved about her cooking. If they could see her the way she looked now, he thought, they'd eat old tires and swear they were being fed filet mignon. "You did fine," he told her. "Don't forget the extra mouths tomorrow."

Rory braced one slim hand on the edge of the door. Her scent, sweet and womanly, rose to embrace him like a lover. What had he been thinking, letting her stay here? He'd be lucky if he got any sleep until she left, and who the hell knew when that would be? It would serve him right if she married Charlie and they both lived here with him.

The picture of her married to Charlie made Travis want to grab her, wrap his fingers in her hair and hold her face still while he branded her mouth with his.

He scrubbed a hand over his own face instead. He was losing it.

"I set my alarm," she volunteered, still standing awkwardly behind the door as if she could wipe out the picture of her that was burned into his brain. "So I guess I'll see you in the morning."

"Yeah. Good night."

"'Night," she echoed. "Sleep well."

He didn't reply. Instead, he went into his room to take his shower—a much colder one than he had been looking forward to.

Through the narrow opening in her doorway, Rory watched his broad back until he disappeared. Then she shut the door quietly before he could come back out and catch her. She was still clutching the bathrobe he'd given her. Without thinking, she rubbed the soft material against her cheek and inhaled. Its only scent was a faint mustiness. Appalled by what she'd done, she hung the robe on a hanger in the closet and climbed back into bed. It seemed like only moments later that the travel alarm on her nightstand went off, waking her from a dream she couldn't quite remember.

Travis was just opening his eyes when he heard the tinny sound of her alarm. Immediately, he imagined her climbing out of bed in her pink pajamas. Big mistake. He never should have touched her, tears or not.

Wearily, he sat up and hung his legs over the side of the bed, rubbing the fatigue from his eyes. It had taken him a long time to go to sleep, and now it was equally hard waking up. He stood and stretched, then he shoved aside the window curtain and looked outside. To the east, the sky was lightening with the promise of dawn. Scratching his chest, he headed for the bathroom.

A little while later, when he'd fastened the snaps on his shirt cuffs and was reaching for his wallet, he spotted the soda can on his dresser. He stared at it thoughtfully, wondering why Rory had been in his room and what she'd say if he asked her.

Chapter Five

When Rory walked into the kitchen, Travis was standing by the sink with a soda can. His presence seemed to fill the big room as he crumpled the can and tossed it in the trash.

When he saw her, he straightened. "Good morning." He had on a blue plaid shirt with his usual brown leather vest and worn jeans. His damp hair was neatly combed, and except for his mustache, his cheeks and jaw were clean shaven.

How would it feel to kiss a man with a mustache?

Rory's cheeks flamed as she stammered out a reply to his greeting. He gave her an odd look, and she was relieved when he began fiddling with the coffee-maker. Then her stomach took an alarming dip as she remembered where she had left her soda can the day before.

Should she say anything, admit she'd been snooping? Tell him she'd just been curious? As if that was any less invasive.

While she dithered, he held up an empty mug. "Coffee?"

"No, thanks." She decided to take the cowardly way out and not mention being in his room. Perhaps he thought the soda can was his. "Would you have any tea?" she asked. Did cowboys drink tea? Probably not.

He frowned thoughtfully. "Yeah, I think so. One of Charlie's—" He broke off abruptly. "We keep it on hand for company. Look in that cannister by the stove. There's a kettle for water in the cupboard." He reached around her as she turned and his bare forearm brushed against her breast. Rory froze and so did he.

Then she pulled away, still tingling from his warmth as he muttered an apology and grabbed the kettle. While he filled it at the sink, Rory fumbled with the tea canister.

Had he felt the same jolt of awareness that she had? She sneaked a look. The back of his neck was red. Perhaps it was only sunburned.

When he set the kettle on the stove, his expression revealed nothing. If not for his apology, she might assume he hadn't even noticed the contact.

Surprised his hands weren't shaking, Travis poured himself some coffee. Blowing on it, he leaned against the counter and watched Rory over the rim of his mug. She was wearing new jeans, a pale yellow knit shirt with a little collar and the same thick-soled athletic shoes she'd had on the day before. Her hair was pulled into a clip, curls escaping and tiny gold hoops dancing at her ears. She studied the contents of the tea canister as if it held the secrets of the universe.

The soft touch of her breast against his arm had been as erotic as anything he could remember. Obviously he needed to get out more.

Only when she'd selected a tea bag and plopped it into her empty mug did she finally look at him. Her eyes were wide, her cheeks stained with color and her lips slightly puckered. She looked as though she'd just been kissed.

Travis took a gulp of hot coffee, and then he latched onto the first thing that came into his mind. "How are your feet?" he asked. "Any blisters?"

She rewarded him with a bright smile. "No. They feel lots better, thanks."

He should have left. There were chores that needed doing before breakfast. Instead, he was tempted to pull out a kitchen chair, straddle it and chew the fat. The fact that nearly a dozen other people would be spending the morning meal with them irritated him to no end.

He needed some air.

"Do you want a ride to the bunkhouse?" he asked abruptly. He didn't want her next to him in the cab of his truck, but good manners insisted he offer.

The sky to the east was just beginning to turn pink. Rory looked out the window as he drank his coffee, unable to take his eyes off her. Confound it, what was it about the woman that hog-tied his tongue and made him hope his brother never came home?

"Looks like a nice day. I'll just walk down after I finish my tea," she said. "Thanks, anyway."

He thought about offering to wait for her and then

discarded the idea. The less time he spent drowning in her blue eyes, hanging on her every word and getting high on her scent, the better off he'd be. He managed to refill his mug without spilling it, unplugged the coffeemaker and grabbed his hat off a peg by the door.

"See you later," he said over his shoulder.

"Have a good day," Rory called out, wondering if she should have gone with him, after all. If he heard her before the door shut behind him, he gave no sign. A moment later, the kettle whistled and she heard the engine of his truck fire up. She was pouring hot water over her tea bag when the phone rang.

Her hand trembled with anticipation as she picked up the receiver. When she heard Charlie's voice, mixed feelings of relief, resentment and hurt flooded through her.

"Where are you? Why are you doing this?" she demanded, cutting through his greeting.

"I guess I didn't really think it out," he replied in a subdued voice. "I'm sorry."

Rory assumed he was referring to the situation between them. "I don't understand. It's not as though we made any promises to each other. There's no pressure on you."

"How are you and Travis getting along?" he asked.

"Travis?" she echoed, puzzled. "How do you think we're getting along? I'm sure the poor man resents having his privacy invaded. I'm not wild about being dumped on him."

"He's not giving you a hard time, is he?"

The question made her realize just how accommodating Travis had been under the circumstances, providing shelter in his own house. Not that she was about to admit anything to Charlie. He deserved to feel guilty. Let him suffer a little. She was getting thoroughly disillusioned with him, anyway. The man she thought she knew didn't even seem to exist.

"It's pretty obvious Travis doesn't like having me here," she told him bluntly. "And I'm uncomfortable around him. After all, he's not you. What did you expect?"

She didn't like him. Outside the open window, Travis turned and walked quietly back to his truck. He'd been coming in to get the gloves he'd forgotten when he heard Rory's voice. He'd meant to make his presence known, but then he'd realized she must be talking to Charlie. Curiosity made him hesitate.

The part about no promises confused him. Wasn't the intent to wed a promise? Then he'd heard the rest of what she said.

He told himself he didn't care. Just because the accidental touch of her breast had shot feeling straight to his groin didn't mean anything—but her lying to him about marrying Charlie did.

Travis climbed back into his truck, shut the door quietly and eased it into gear. Fall roundup started today. He'd be too busy to even think about her.

All through breakfast, Rory watched for an opportunity to tell Travis about the phone call. When he first walked in, he was deep in conversation with Wes and two men she hadn't seen before. By the time everyone was finished eating, including a couple more newcomers, she was busy making sandwiches for the men's lunches. When she glanced up, Travis was headed toward the door with Steve and Gus.

Rory hurried after them. "Could I talk to you for a minute?" she called after Travis.

When he turned reluctantly, his expression was closed, his eyes edged with ice. "Can't it wait? We've got a big day ahead of us."

Rory glanced at Steve and Gus, who were watching them with undisguised curiosity. If Travis couldn't be bothered to give her a minute, she wasn't going to push herself on him. Charlie's call could wait.

"It's not important." Frustrated, she headed back to the waiting piles of sandwich fixings.

As soon as Travis had walked out the door, Jane came over, wiping her soapy hands on her apron.

"Wow," she said. "Travis is sure in a bad mood this morning."

Rory shrugged and began loading dirty plates into the dishwasher. "He's the boss," she said. "I guess he can act any way he wants."

"Maybe he's upset about his brother," Jane said in a conspiratorial tone. "Let me tell you, the rumors are flyin' thick and fast."

Rory glanced around uneasily, not wanting to be caught gossiping. "You mean Adam?" she asked innocently. "What's he done?"

Jane crossed her arms. "No, the younger one, Charlie. Guess you haven't met him yet. That boy's always making mischief of some kind or other."

Rory's spirits sank. She'd thought Charlie was such a rock. Sad to see her judgment where men were concerned hadn't improved since she'd first believed

Daniel Mancini would settle down if she married him. "What kind of mischief?" she asked.

Jane sidled closer and lowered her voice. "The rumor going around now is that he's up and eloped."

Travis tried all day to get out of his head the words he'd overheard Rory say. No matter how many cows he flushed out of the brush, no matter how many stragglers he herded, no matter how many skittish calves he brought in to join the growing number of animals to be sorted, treated and sold, no matter how much energy or sweat he expended, he couldn't banish the memory.

She didn't like him.

He wouldn't consider himself a deeply analytical man, nor did he dwell overmuch on his popularity with the opposite sex. He'd learned years ago that women were attracted to men who could charm them, make them laugh and discuss feelings he'd always kept private. He had never possessed those talents and he had no clue how to acquire them. Growing up without any women in the household, he'd never learned how to relax around them.

Rory was no exception. She exasperated him, she intrigued him, most of all she tied him in knots. Why would a woman with her looks and tenacity travel all this way for a man she'd never met? A man who'd apparently made her no promises.

Why would she lie about marrying him?

Travis had no answers.

This afternoon he was driving a jeep, although he preferred riding horseback. He'd had to replace some rotted posts on a section of fence that had gone down, and now he was bouncing across one of the empty pastures when he noticed riders to the west bringing in a small group of cows with their calves.

Steve waved his hat and Travis lifted a hand in response. When Steve waved again, Travis pulled over and waited. Immediately Steve said something to the others and separated from the group at an easy walk. Only then did Travis notice that his horse was limping.

"You headed back?" Steve asked when he was in shouting distance.

"Yeah. What's wrong with Jingle?"

Steve dismounted and led the horse to the jeep. "He picked up a rock. I got it out, but his foot's bruised. No point in making it any worse. Can you give me a lift?"

Travis wasn't in the mood for company, especially Steve's. He tended to chatter like an old woman. Still, there was no good reason to refuse. "Sure," he said. "Throw his saddle in the jeep and hitch him to the back." There were a couple of things he'd meant to take care of when he got in, but now it would take them until supper to reach the stable.

Once Steve was settled, they traveled for a few moments in relative silence. Steve made several comments about the cattle they'd rounded up that day. As Travis scanned the line of fence for any more signs of trouble, all he had to contribute to the conversation was an occasional grunt. Then Steve glanced at him and scratched nervously at the baby fuzz on his chin.

Travis tensed. What was on his mind? Immediately, Travis thought of Rory. Steve had certainly been friendly toward her. If he asked, what should Travis tell him?

Most of the men had learned it was easier to face down a rattler than to ask him anything personal; Steve wasn't one of them. Like a big puppy, he barged in where more cautious dogs wouldn't dare tread.

"I heard Charlie got married," Steve said. "That he eloped."

Travis swerved abruptly, narrowly missing a fence post. Behind them, Steve's horse whinnied in protest. "Is that so?" Travis drawled. Damn, he should have known Charlie's absence would be noticed, commented on. Speculated about.

Steve cleared his throat, obviously taking his rhetorical question as an invitation to proceed. "No one seems to know where he's gone," he continued in a rush. "But it must be something pretty important for him to leave right before roundup."

Travis kept driving, kept inspecting fence. He had no intention of discussing the situation with Steve or anyone else.

After a few moments, his passenger shifted in the seat. He turned to glance at his horse. "Just thought you'd like to know what the men are saying, that's all," he mumbled before he finally lapsed into blessed silence.

After a moment, Travis decided to take pity on him. "I think I can safely tell you that Charlie hasn't gotten married."

Steve's head snapped back around. "Is that right? I said I didn't think he was seeing anyone, but Gus, you know how stubborn he can be, like a dog with a bone, he said it would have to be something like that for Charlie to miss roundup.'' He hesitated, Adam's apple bobbing as he swallowed. ''You probably know what's going on, right?''

Travis thought about crossing his fingers. ''I probably do, yeah.''

His lapse into conversation must have given the young cowhand a jolt of courage. He grinned through the layer of dust on his face.

''The other rumor flying around thicker 'n flies on a three-day-old carcass is that new redheaded cook, Rory, is shacked up with you.''

Travis felt his ears go hot with embarrassment. ''She's staying at my house,'' he blurted, ''but there's nothing going on.'' Damn, what was wrong with him? He didn't owe Steve an explanation.

''Uh-huh.'' Steve's grin was knowing. ''Way to go, boss. She's a real fox.''

Travis nearly groaned with disgust. ''We needed a cook,'' he said shortly, holding on to his temper with difficulty. ''She needed a place to stay. End of story. The next man I hear spreading rumors will answer to me.'' He didn't care what the men said about him, but Rory didn't deserve this kind of speculation. Her personal life was no one else's business.

He remembered how he had eavesdropped on her and shifted guiltily in the seat.

Steve must have realized he was less than pleased, because he didn't say anything more about it.

On Friday morning when breakfast was done, Rory was putting butter and milk back into the bigger of the two refrigerators in the bunkhouse kitchen when

Travis approached her. For the last couple of days he'd been keeping his distance, and she had herself convinced she liked that just fine.

"Wes will cook supper tomorrow," he said. "Go ahead and make out a supply list, and then in the morning you and Jane can go to town after breakfast."

"Okay," Rory replied as she wiped off the counter. She didn't look at him, but she was acutely aware of his nearness.

As far as she knew, no one had heard from Charlie since he'd called her two days ago, and she never did tell Travis. In the mornings he left the house before she went downstairs; in the evenings she was in her room when he got home and she didn't venture out. She'd learned the hard way to listen at her door before she opened it. Luckily she'd brought a couple of paperbacks with her. She remembered with a bitter little smile that she'd packed them thinking she wouldn't have the time to read.

Jane walked over to where they were standing. "I can't take Rory to town tomorrow," she said. "I've got a dentist appointment in Limon. I'd postpone it, but my tooth's really been bothering me." She opened her mouth and pointed to the back.

"Don't worry about it," Travis said. "I shouldn't have assumed you'd be available." He gave her a smile that made Rory blink.

Apparently it affected Jane as well. Her cheeks went pink and she put a hand on one skinny hip. "Everyone helps out during roundup," she replied. "Normally, I wouldn't mind at all." Her gaze flicked to Rory and back again. ''Why don't you drive her?'' she suggested to him with an arch expression.

Rory straightened abruptly, and Travis shot her a startled glance, as if he'd forgotten she was there.

''Travis must be busy—'' Rory began.

''I'll find someone—'' he said at the same time.

They both stopped and looked at each other with embarrassed expressions. Rory remained silent, determined to squelch Jane's matchmaking ideas as soon as they were alone. Still, if Travis didn't want anything to do with her, he could make the explanations.

''That would probably be the best idea,'' he conceded, surprising her.

Only when Rory gaped at him did the smallest flicker of a smile tease the corners of his mouth. Then his expression sobered. ''Don't forget to make out a supply list,'' he said, and then he left.

Immediately, Rory turned to Jane, who wore a smug grin. ''You don't have to thank me,'' she said with a wave of her hand. ''I'm going out for a smoke.''

''Thank you!'' Rory sputtered at her departing back, glad they were alone. ''For what?''

Jane swaggered to the door. ''I can see what's going on between the two of you,'' she called. ''I'm just helping things along.''

Rory was too irritated to reply. Maybe Jane fancied that she could see something, but Rory sure as heck couldn't. All she knew was that Travis resented having her here more than ever and her own attraction to him was growing every day.

Damn you, Charlie, she thought as Jane went out

the door, strutting like a runway model, *you'd better get home before we kill each other.*

"Could you drop me at the drugstore?" Rory asked as she and Travis turned onto the main street of Waterloo the next morning. "There are a few personal items I need." Of all the things she might have forgotten to pack, these had to be the most awkward to buy when one had to hitch a ride to town with a macho cowboy who also happened to be a bachelor.

"I'll come in with you," he replied. "I need some razor blades." He glanced at her and must have read something of her dismay in her expression, despite the shield of her sunglasses. "Or I, uh, could run another errand and just meet you at the grocery store," he added lamely. Pink ran along his jawline, and his attention shot back to the road with unflattering haste.

"Thank you, that will be fine," she said quietly. He'd confirmed to her at breakfast that he would be the one taking her to town, and he hadn't looked happy about it. Still didn't.

Jane hadn't been there this morning to crow about her meddling. A teenage boy had showed up to bus dishes instead, so at least Rory hadn't had to deal with her smug "I told you so" expression. The boy, named Mike, reminded Rory of her nephews, Daniel's sister's boys, who'd worked in the diner before and after school and on weekends. The diner had been a family business, her ex-husband's family. Rory had meant to quit after their divorce, but she'd never gotten around to it and five more years had drifted by without her notice.

All during the drive to town this morning, she had been painfully aware of Travis a couple of feet away from her in the cab of the truck. He was wearing a dressier shirt than usual, with red-and-white stripes and pearl snaps, dark blue Wrangler jeans and polished black boots she hadn't seen before. His belt buckle was a large oval of shiny silver. His aftershave smelled of piney woods and fresh air, and his cowboy hat was tan instead of black.

Apparently going to town for groceries was an event around here, she thought with a silent chuckle. Then she glanced at her own attire.

She, too, was wearing dark blue jeans, although they were a different brand from his. With them she had paired a long-sleeved blue chambray shirt she'd bought back in New York because she'd thought at the time it looked Western. The shirt had small white flowers embroidered on the collar, the cuffs and across the back of the yoke. If Travis thought she looked nice, he hadn't said. He'd barely glanced at her, but she'd noticed a muscle jump along his jawline. Maybe he was worried about the roundup.

"Would you like to have lunch at the café before we do the shopping?" he asked, startling her.

Her surprise must have shown, because he added almost defensively, "I thought you might like a change from your own cooking."

"Uh, that would be nice," she stammered. "If you can spare the time."

For a moment, the steely look in his eyes softened. "I'll make the time."

Travis realized he was staring at Rory like a lovesick calf. He could hardly help himself. She was so pretty in jeans and a blue shirt, which turned her eyes dark and mysterious. Even in casual clothes, she had an air of sophistication that both attracted and dismayed him. She was like no woman he'd ever known.

Immediately, he brought himself up short. What was he thinking about? He knew less about her now than he had days ago. Until Charlie chose to enlighten him, he'd better keep the reluctant attraction he felt toward her under strict control.

Rory chose that moment to smile at him. His common sense went the way of high beef prices and his blood surged in mindless response.

"Hey!" someone shouted, snapping his attention back to the street. To his embarrassment, one of the old codgers who were usually settled on the post office porch was crossing in front of the truck.

"Watch where you're going, Winchester," he yelled. "I ain't ready to pack it in yet."

"Sorry, Clyde," Travis replied through his open window.

The old man leaned on his cane and peered past him at Rory. As Travis drove on by, ignoring him, he tipped his hat to her. She smiled in return. Soon it would be all over town that she'd been with Travis.

"Who was that?" she asked.

"Clyde Burrows. He's been around since the Ice Age. Used to own the barber shop. Now he fancies himself and his cronies as the watchdogs of Waterloo," Travis replied dryly.

Rory laughed. "We had a couple of guys like him back home. They were a fixture in front porch rockers, and they knew what was going on in the neighborhood almost before it happened."

"Where'd you get a name like Mancini?" Travis asked, curious about her background. "You don't look Italian." Not with that red hair and those freckles. He wondered if she had more of the coppery dots, like a sprinkle of cinnamon sugar, in places that didn't show.

She glanced away. "Mancini was my ex's name."

She was divorced. Immediately he wondered what had gone wrong. Had she loved her husband? Had he hurt her? Maybe she'd left him. "Why'd you keep the name?" he asked. Was she carrying a torch?

"I never cared for my maiden name," she replied. "Mancini was the lesser of two evils."

"What's your maiden name?" he asked, parking the truck on the main street. He recognized Donovan Buchanan's pickup and wondered what the other rancher was doing in Waterloo. He and Travis had become friends through the local cattlemen's association several years before.

Rory chuckled as he shut off the engine. "I'm not telling."

Distracted, Travis shrugged. "Suit yourself." He got out of his truck, grabbed their jackets from behind the seat and joined Rory on the sidewalk. "Drugstore's right down there." He pointed. "I'll wait for you at Emma's." He was already regretting the invitation to lunch, but there was no way to take it back without embarrassing both of them.

While they stood on the sidewalk, two people he knew from church walked by and eyeballed Rory curiously. Even dressed the way she was, in a casual shirt, jeans and her new boots, her red hair and statuesque figure drew attention. Travis shifted uneasily and tugged his hat farther down over his eyes, as if that would hide him from the speculative glances they were getting.

"Anything I can pick up for you?" she asked.

He shook his head. The razor blades could wait, and the last time he'd purchased condoms at a drugstore, he'd driven to a neighboring town where he was less well-known. There had been snow on the ground then, and now it was September already.

No wonder he couldn't get this woman's image out of his dreams. It had nothing to do with feelings he didn't understand; good old-fashioned lust was wrecking his sleep, plain and simple.

"I'll just be a few minutes," Rory said.

As she walked away, Travis made a pretense of checking his tires while he watched to make sure she found the drugstore. The sidewalk wasn't crowded, but the men walking toward her parted like the Red Sea. Several Stetsons were raised in polite salute as she passed, and two cowhands Travis knew by sight turned to mark her progress after she'd gone by.

He couldn't blame them. From the rear, as from the front, she was worth watching. Her hips swayed gently. Her hair bobbed. Her long legs—

From the street a horn honked, breaking his concentration. Annoyed at himself, Travis crossed to the café. When he walked inside and sat in a corner booth, Hazel brought him a menu.

"How's the woman who was with you the other day?" she asked as she poured his coffee. "Feeling better?"

It took Travis a moment to remember that Rory had been shaky from the heat then. Today the temperature was thirty degrees cooler. "She's fine," he said shortly, and then he picked up the menu and studied it as if he didn't already have its contents memorized.

Hazel took the hint and left him alone.

"You must be new in town," remarked the girl who rang up Rory's purchases at the drugstore. Her dark hair was streaked with brassy blond, her nails were painted black, and she was chewing gum. "Monica" was typed on her name tag in faint letters.

"I'm staying at the Winchester spread," Rory replied. Except for some of the products it carried, the little store could have been transported from the century before. The floors were wood, as were the shelves and glass-fronted display cases. There was a potbellied stove in one corner. Everywhere, an astonishing variety of merchandise was crammed, tucked and stacked, from rows of toothpaste, aspirin and first aid supplies to displays of baseball caps and sunglasses. There were postcards and umbrellas, saddle soap and fry pans. Skeins of yarn sat next to boxes of canning jars. On the counter beside a modern cash register was a rack of bolero ties and one of earrings made from feathers, beads and bits of polished wood.

Monica cocked her head as she handed back Rory's change. "Where are you from?"

"New York," Rory admitted, pocketing the money carefully.

Monica's eyes grew round and she quit chewing the gum. "Wow. I always wanted to go there, to look around, you know. Maybe to make a career out of acting or singing." She waved her black-tipped fingers in an all-encompassing gesture. "Nothing ever happens around here. You know what I'm saying?'' She glanced around, and then she leaned forward as she handed Rory a plastic bag with her purchases. ''You know, I've been stuck in Waterloo *all my life.*''

Rory smiled. The girl looked maybe seventeen. ''Perhaps you'll still get to see the world,'' she said. ''You've got a few good years left.''

Monica looked puzzled. She worked her gum for a moment. ''Yeah,'' she said finally. ''I guess.''

Moments later, Rory held the gaping edges of her jacket around her as she tossed the bag containing her feminine supplies in the truck. The wind was chilly and it smelled of fall. Back home the nights would be getting colder, the days losing their heat and humidity as winter crept closer. The leaves would be turning, the flowers dying.

She hesitated, picturing the diner as she'd last seen it, the windows boarded up, the shutters and door trim already being stripped away in the first steps of the remodeling that would transform the old neighborhood business into a trendy new coffee bar. As she stepped off the curb, her eyes swam with tears in silent mourning for the feeling of family, of belonging, that was gone and couldn't be replaced.

A squeal of tires shattered the image clouding her vision. A horn blared, a man shouted a warning, and, from the sidewalk behind her, a woman screamed.

Chapter Six

From inside the café, Travis heard the squeal of brakes. He looked out the window and his coffee mug crashed to the table. He was out the door before he realized he'd gotten to his feet.

A pickup was stopped in the street, dust swirling around it, and Rory was sprawled in a heap on the ground. Rushing to her side, Travis barely saw the driver of the truck.

"Rory!" he exclaimed as he crouched over her, heart thundering in his chest. "Are you okay?"

Her eyes were open, lashes fluttering. Relieved, he grabbed a breath and took her hand. Her head popped up and her gaze collided with his.

"I'm fine." Her hair stuck out wildly in all directions, and she was so pale the freckles across her nose stood out.

"Don't move her," someone said when she struggled to sit up.

Travis touched her cheek with a hand that trembled. "Where are you hurt?"

She pushed herself up on her elbows and glanced at the small group of people who had gathered around them. "I'm okay," she repeated.

He curled a hand over the delicate bones of her shoulder. "Stay still," he told her. "We'll get help." At least he didn't see any blood.

"Is she okay?" a woman asked, waving a cellular phone. "Shall I call the doctor?"

"Thank you, but I don't need a doctor," Rory replied.

"I didn't hit her," a husky voice said from behind Travis. "I never hit her."

Travis barely turned his head. "Why weren't you watching where you were going?"

"I was," the man protested. "She stepped right in front of my truck."

"He's right." Rory pushed Travis's hand away as she sat up. "He didn't hit me. I fell trying to get out of his way, that's all."

Travis gaped at her. Her cheeks were flushed, her gaze downcast. He rocked back on his heels.

"You fell? That's all?" He'd run over here as if someone had just shot his best horse. He glanced at the café, where Hazel and several others were looking out the window.

"I'm sorry if I scared you." Rory's gaze lifted to his chest and her eyes widened. "Oh, dear."

He looked down at his shirt, noticing for the first time that he'd spilled coffee all over the front of it.

''Are you okay, miss?'' asked Roy Templeton, who ran the boot repair shop. He leaned over her, hands fluttering like those of a fussy old woman.

Rory nodded. ''Yes, thank you.'' She tried getting to her feet.

''She was just in the drugstore,'' said a young girl Travis thought was one of the Malones' brood. She'd done something awful to her hair. ''The lady walked right out in front of that truck.'' Her voice rose, her jaw working with rapid-fire movements. ''She could have been killed. Wow.''

For a moment, reaction curdled Travis's gut like sour milk. Finally people began drifting away, the crisis over. He straightened and helped Rory up. Had she seen the way he'd bolted out of the café? Probably not. She was too busy falling down and scaring the hell out of him.

Ducking her head, she slapped the dust off her jeans. ''I feel like an idiot,'' she mumbled.

A car drove past slowly, the teenage driver hanging out the window.

''What happened?'' he called over the blare of his radio.

''Nothing,'' snapped the driver who'd nearly hit Rory. ''Just move on.''

''I'm sorry,'' she told him. ''It was my fault.''

His hand went to the brim of his baseball cap. ''No, ma'am, don't you worry. As long as you're not hurt.''

''Just my pride,'' she replied, with a smile that Travis wished she'd directed at him—and not because he'd nearly run her down.

What was he thinking?

"Perhaps I should give you my name, just in case," the other man suggested.

"That won't be necessary," Travis replied. "She'll be fine. I'll see to her."

The driver looked down at a heavy gold watch on his wrist. "If you're sure," he said. "I do have an appointment."

"Yes, thanks for stopping." Rory was staring as if he'd done something wonderful. Well, he couldn't very well have driven over her.

"She's fine." Travis was acutely conscious of Roy Templeton and the Malone girl watching from the sidewalk. "Don't let us keep you," he told the driver. "Your truck's blocking traffic." As if Main Street in Waterloo was downtown L.A. What was rush hour, two cars in a row?

With a last concerned glance at Rory, the other man tipped his hat again, hitched up his jeans and finally left. Rory stuck her fingers into her hair and fluffed it, making it stick out more than it had. Dirt smudged her cheek. Travis wanted to lick his handkerchief and wipe away the spot, but he resisted. His heartbeat was almost back to normal. Touching her might get it going again. All he could think about was the way she'd looked sprawled in the street like a broken doll. That and the surge of emotion that had pumped through him when he found out she hadn't been hit.

Roy and the girl went back inside. The pickup drove by slowly, the driver lifting his hand in a good-bye salute. Rory waved back.

"You sure you're okay?" Travis asked gruffly.

When she heard the edge of annoyance to his voice, Rory felt her cheeks go hot all over again. Too bad he'd been a witness to the embarrassing fiasco. She felt like such a klutz. "I'd just like to get out of here," she said, looking around. At least everyone else had finally left. "Can we pick up the supplies and go?"

"What about lunch?" he asked.

She shrugged. "I'm not really hungry." She glanced over at the café. It was too much to hope that the people inside hadn't noticed the commotion she'd caused.

Travis stared down at her for a long moment. His gray eyes were darker than she'd ever seen them, and his expression was even more forbidding than usual. No doubt he was annoyed by all the fuss.

He glanced up and down the street. "Okay," he said finally. "Let's go."

"Honey, are you okay?" the waitress from the café called from across the street.

"Yes, thanks." Rory waggled her fingers in response.

"Emma says for you to come and have some lunch on the house. You, too, Travis." She waited in the doorway expectantly.

He looked even more annoyed. "She'll stand there and yell until we agree."

"Okay." With a sigh and a last futile swipe at her dirty jeans, Rory looked carefully up and down the street and then she led the way across.

Travis hadn't said much at the café when several other patrons came by their booth and asked if she was all right, even when two women introduced themselves to Rory and greeted him by name. At the grocery store afterward he'd been all business, and on the way back to the ranch he'd driven in silence.

Rory's elbow hurt where she'd banged it, and she was worn out emotionally from the fuss and the embarrassment. Her hair felt itchy from the dust of the street, and she could swear she tasted grit in her mouth, even after the glass of iced tea she'd drunk with lunch.

By the time they'd unloaded the supplies at the bunkhouse and driven back to Travis's, her fatigue had turned to exasperation. ''Are you mad at me for what happened back in town?'' she demanded as soon as they'd walked into his kitchen, ''or just disappointed that your problem wasn't eliminated by that pickup truck?''

Travis swung around and stared, sending prickles of alarm up her spine. ''What do you mean?'' he growled.

It was too late to retreat, and Rory was pushed past discretion. ''If he'd hit me, I might be out of your hair for good,'' she blurted, facing him and thrusting up her chin. ''No more boarder, no more brother's intended. I think you'd like that.''

Something in Travis's eyes blazed, and he closed the space between them in two strides. ''You want to know what I'd like?'' he asked, voice low and deadly. ''I'll show you.''

Before Rory could guess what he intended, he caught her face in his hands and lowered his head. She was barely aware of his fingers digging into her scalp. His nearness swamped her senses, scattered her wits, and then his hot, seeking mouth covered hers in a punishing kiss.

Her initial spurt of fear was swamped by the lust that rippled through her at the touch of his lips. Her head spun. Her stomach pitched and her knees buckled. She moaned, deep in her throat, and clutched at his wide shoulders to keep from falling.

His arms tightened as he gathered her closer, and his lips softened on hers. His tongue sought entrance, wooed, seduced and melded. She buried her fingers in the hair at the back of his neck. Her thumb brushed his jaw, rasped against his whiskers. The pure masculinity of his size, his bulk, his heat and his hard, rough textures threatened to pull her under. Into a dark river of passion.

Before she'd sampled nearly enough of him, he broke the kiss and stared intently, chest heaving. His eyes were narrowed, burning. Wanting more, she tipped back her head and made a wordless sound of need in her throat. Travis groaned and kissed her again. His tongue caressed her lips and she opened to him, greedy for more of his taste. He lifted her off the floor and crushed her closer. Beneath her hands, the muscles of his shoulders were iron hard.

Rory's arms encircled his neck and she clung. He changed the angle of the kiss and his hat fell to the floor.

The dull thud must have broken the spell. He lifted his head, buried his face in her hair and sucked in a ragged breath. She felt him shudder. He lowered her until her feet touched the floor, and then his arms fell away.

"I'm sorry," he gasped, face averted. He bent down and picked up his hat, slapping it against his thigh.

Rory swayed and grabbed hold of the counter. She blinked several times, and then she raised tentative fingers to her throbbing lips. They were swollen and exquisitely sensitized.

"Wow," she muttered softly.

Travis glanced back over his shoulder. The skin stretched taut over his cheekbones was flushed a dusky red. "It won't happen again." His voice was rough, as if he'd been shouting. "I don't want you to worry."

She nearly told him she was more worried that he wouldn't kiss her again. Instead, she studied his profile as she tried to sort through the emotions rioting inside her.

Emotions he'd raised with his kiss.

"You weren't the only one involved here," she began. "I share the responsibility with you."

He was already shaking his head. "You're staying in my house, under my care. I have to protect you, even from myself."

Rory could only stare. What century had he sprung from? "And if I don't want to be protected?"

Travis turned to face her, and his gaze flicked to her mouth as if he couldn't help himself. She felt the visual caress as if he'd kissed her again. "It's not up to you," he stated flatly.

With that, he strode out the back door. Moments later, she heard his truck start. Damn the man, to leave her churned up like this while he walked away as if nothing had happened.

Perhaps, to his way of thinking, nothing had. While she was pacing, arms folded across her chest as if to keep her thudding heart from exploding, Rory realized she hadn't thought of Charlie once when she'd been in Travis's arms.

As if on cue, the phone rang. Distracted, she picked it up. "Winchester's."

"Rory?" It was Charlie's voice.

Her fingers tightened on the receiver. "You'd better get back here and fast," she cried.

"What's happened? Are you okay?"

She drew in a steadying breath. "I warned you that Travis and I weren't getting along. My being here just isn't working. If you aren't coming back, I'm leaving," she threatened, past caring.

"Slow down, honey," Charlie urged. "Tell me what's the matter."

What was Rory supposed to say? *He kissed me, and I'm scared.* Not bloody likely. "This is crazy," she told him instead. "I'm working here as a camp cook and you're God-knows-where on vacation."

"I'll come back, I promise," Charlie said in a soothing voice. "Will you wait?"

"How long?" she asked. "When are you coming back?"

"Soon."

Frustration wiped away what little patience she had left. "That's not good enough." Scrubbing at the angry tears that had filled her eyes and were spilling onto her cheeks, she slammed down the receiver, cutting off his reply.

She walked into the bunkhouse kitchen the next morning, still exhausted from the nearly sleepless night she'd spent waiting to hear Travis's footsteps on the stairs, footsteps that never came. Now the first thing she saw was a bearded little man who reminded her of the cook from old "Rawhide" reruns. He was slicing potatoes energetically. When she walked in, he looked up and smiled without missing a stroke.

"You must be Rory," he said. "'Tall, gorgeous redhead' doesn't fit many people around this place."

Despite her bad mood, Rory couldn't help but return his grin with one of her own. A big pan of cinnamon rolls waited to go into the oven, and a platter of sliced ham sat on the counter.

"And you must be my fairy godfather," she countered.

He stopped cutting long enough to extend a wrinkled hand with part of one finger missing. "Arnold Flynn, at your service. Call me Flynn. Want some coffee?"

Rory helped herself to a mug of dark brew that smelled like heaven. "So, am I out of a job?" she asked lightly. The kitchen looked as though Flynn had breakfast well under control. Now what was she supposed to do?

He glanced up, the knife flashing, and she figured she knew how he'd lost the tip of that finger. "I could use some help," he said, "at least until roundup is over."

She grabbed her apron off the hook by the door, fatigue forgotten. "What would you like me to do first?"

Later, when the men filed in for breakfast, they all came over to greet Flynn. Even Adam showed up to welcome him back and inquire about the sister Flynn had gone to care for.

"She pulled through the surgery fine, and we found

a nice woman to stay with her, so I came back earlier than I expected,'' Flynn replied to his query. ''Didn't know I'd been replaced so handily.''

Rory made a gesture of protest. ''Only temporarily. I could never fill your, er, boots.'' She was touched when Wes, Steve and Barney made a point to tell her how much they had enjoyed her cooking.

''And she's a damn sight easier on the eyes than you,'' Wes told Flynn as the cook flipped pancakes on the grill.

''Bet she don't fix prairie oysters like I do, though,'' Flynn retorted, waving his spatula.

Rory had an idea what prairie oysters were, the by-product of converting young bull calves to steers. Her cheeks grew warm when the men eyed her expectantly, but she refrained from commenting. Just then, Jane came in and immediately rushed over to give Flynn a hug.

''Perhaps you'll have time to see some of the roundup, now that Cookie's back,'' Steve suggested, a toothpick dancing from one side of his mouth to the other.

Before Rory could reply, Adam spoke up. ''Good idea. You might find what we do interesting. Do you ride?''

With mixed feelings, Rory shook her head. '''Fraid not. Growing up in the Bronx, I didn't have a lot of opportunity.'' There had been riding stables around, of course, but they were way too pricey for her family.

She didn't want to get in anyone's way while she was here, especially Travis's. He hadn't returned to the house at all after he'd kissed her, and she figured he must have slept in the bunkhouse rather than spend the night under the same roof as her. She would like to check out the workings of a real ranch, though. What little she'd seen so far was fascinating.

''No matter,'' Adam said. ''You can ride in the jeep.''

Just then, Travis walked in, glancing at the group around Flynn, and saluted the cook with his empty mug before he crossed to the big coffee urn. When he would have gone over to the table and sat down, Adam called out to him.

''Flynn's back,'' he said unnecessarily. ''We were just saying that Rory should see some of the roundup, now that she won't be cooking full-time.''

Distress curled like razor wire in her stomach as she discerned the direction of Adam's remarks. Why was everyone so eager to push her at Travis? Helpless, she fisted her hands beneath the protective cover of her apron and muttered a silent plea.

His expression grew wary while Adam's remained patently innocent. ''Since you're going to be in the yard most of the day, why don't you give her a tour after breakfast?''

Travis frowned and Rory muffled a groan. Ignoring her, he pulled out his usual chair and sat down. He took a leisurely sip of his coffee. ''I have work to do,'' he told Adam. ''I won't have time to baby-sit a greenhorn.''

Rory stepped forward, an angry protest on the tip of her tongue. Before she could voice it, Adam forestalled her with a hand on her arm. ''Sure you do. She won't be that much trouble, will you, Rory?'' His green eyes danced as he watched her, and his grin was mischievous. For some reason she couldn't fathom, his smile, so like Travis's, didn't affect her in nearly the same way.

If he was using her to annoy his brother, he was succeeding. Travis wore a scowl a lesser man might have found intimidating. She resented being a pawn between siblings, but the chance to see a real roundup *and* to spend time with Travis, even time he resented, was too great a lure.

"I don't want to bother him when he's busy," she protested halfheartedly.

"Nonsense." Adam waved a hand in airy dismissal. "The two of you can work out when he'll be back to pick you up." His voice had taken on an edge of quiet authority that apparently even his younger brother wasn't used to questioning. Instead, Travis bent his head and studied his mug as if he found the contents fascinating.

Adam winked at Rory, who could only dredge up a faint smile in reply, and then he circled the counter. Slapping Flynn on the back, he left, and the rest of the men, realizing the show was over, took their places at the table.

Rory repositioned the cowboy hat Travis had brought with him and insisted she wear, and braced her booted feet on the bottom rung of the fence. Overhead the sky was bright blue, but a breeze reminded her that summer was past and days like today were to be savored.

Tipping back her head, she took a deep, bracing breath of the clean air and sighed with contentment. Charlie was gone, her life was in turmoil, and Travis was ignoring her. Yet something in the atmosphere of this wide-open land acted as a balm to her soul. Her other problems, the ones she'd tried to leave behind, seemed far away indeed.

"You okay?" Steve asked from horseback in the corral before her. "Can I get you anything?" Like several of the other men, he'd removed his shirt to reveal a torso that was tanned and fit. The temperature, which was comfortable for sitting, was no doubt less so for hard physical work.

Rory smiled at Steve. He was a nice kid. "Thanks, but I'm fine." She could have used a cold drink, but the last thing she wanted was for Travis to see her distracting one of the men from his duties.

Watching the procedure for the last hour, she'd been able to slowly make sense of it. When Travis had first left her perched on the fence with instructions to stay put, Steve had come over and explained that for the past week they'd been rounding up the steers and heifers that were being sold. A truck would be here in less than an hour to transport them to market. The calves would be weaned and held over till spring. That accounted for the anxious bawling she could hear from the pens.

As men on horseback separated the animals and herded them into different pens, Rory's gaze remained fixed on Travis. He hadn't removed his shirt. His clothes and hat were covered with the dust that rose in clouds around the horses and the cattle that seemed bent on resisting every effort to send them where they were supposed to go. Luckily for Rory, the dust was so far being blown away from her.

Despite his obviously foul mood, Travis had been

thoughtful enough to give the jeep keys to her so she could leave if the dust, heat and noise got to be too much. Those had been his words; Rory couldn't imagine growing tired of the spectacle unfolding before her.

As a child she'd seen a rodeo once in Madison Square Garden. Her parents, who had both died months apart right after she'd married Daniel, had taken her. The family outing was one of many fond memories of her childhood. Her parents had almost given up on having a child by the time she was born. Her father had been a television repairman, but not an especially successful one; her mother had been a housewife. They'd both seemed happy that Rory's marriage brought her both love and financial security. Part of her was relieved they hadn't lived to see her lose first one and then the other.

A shout brought her back to the present. A black-and-white cow had apparently bolted from her appointed path at the last moment. Travis, riding a big gray horse, streaked after the animal while Rory watched, fascinated. After a series of moves and countermoves, the cow gave up and headed peacefully toward the gate. Ignoring a whoop from Barney, Travis rode over to the fence and leaned down to open an ice chest. While Rory indulged herself and studied him, he stripped off his shirt, revealing powerful bronzed shoulders and arms.

She swallowed dryly as he dunked a bandanna into the ice chest and brought it back dripping wet to skim his bare skin. Rivulets of water ran down his chest to disappear beneath his wide leather belt. She'd been right about him; his build made a mockery of the men who worked out to attain physical perfection.

Finally, while she continued to stare, barely aware of the noise from the cattle and the shouts of the other ranch hands, he leaned back down and fished out two cans of soda from the chest. For a moment, he held one against the side of his neck while she swallowed and did her best to ignore her own dry mouth. Then he surprised her by heading his horse in her direction.

While he rode slowly toward her, Rory gripped the top rail of her perch hard and wished she could fan her burning cheeks. At least he had no idea she'd been watching him as avidly as a green boy at a strip club. She'd barely had time to compose herself when he drew up in front of her, popped the top on one dripping soda can and held it out.

"Thanks," she managed to say, her gaze riveted on his face as she accepted the drink. Her fingers brushed his leather work glove. She was afraid if her attention wandered to the rest of him, he'd see the naked lust on her face, as easy to read as a neon sign on a clear prairie night.

"Are you bored yet?" he asked. "You can go back to the house if you want." His nose was sunburned; his face was caked with dirt and sweat. His chest was streaked with it, and his jeans and boots looked as though he'd been caught in a desert dust storm. Flies buzzed around his horse despite the constant swish of its tail. When Travis tucked the other soda can under his arm and removed his hat, his hair was plastered to his head. He was the most attractive man Rory had ever seen.

"I'm not the least bit bored," she replied truthfully. "I could watch this for days."

Travis braced one hand on his thigh and looked around. His horse sidestepped, and the saddle creaked beneath him. The bridle jingled. "It would get old before too long," he said with maddening certainty.

She chose not to argue. "I should get over to the kitchen and help Flynn with supper." Her gaze skimmed his chest. As soon as she realized what she was doing, she took a large swallow of soda and promptly choked on it.

"Easy," he said, a frown of concern pleating his forehead while he watched her intently.

Eyes streaming, Rory croaked out a weak, "I'm all right," then took another tiny sip of soda. She managed to stop coughing long enough to blot her eyes with a tissue from her pocket. Travis took the soda can and held it while she blew her nose.

"Don't worry about Flynn," he told her as he handed back her drink. "The man's in his element with his pots and pans, and he has Jane to help him. Besides, you've earned an afternoon off."

"Now that he's back, I'll have to figure out another way to earn my keep until Charlie decides to come home," she said, watching Travis closely.

He shrugged, looking irritated. "Clean the house if you feel like it," he suggested. "It could probably use a good going over, and there's plenty of dirty laundry, if you aren't above doing it."

"Of course I'm not," she replied. "But what about after that?"

Travis looked at her for a moment that spun out between them. Was he wondering how long she'd stay, waiting for a man who apparently didn't want to come home? "After that, I guess we'll see," he said enigmatically.

Rory hung her head, obviously disappointed by his reply. What did she want him to say? That Charlie would be coming back any day? Travis didn't know if he even believed that anymore. That she could stay as long as she wanted? How much more of her presence under his roof each night could his control take?

What would she say if he admitted his sleep was laced with dreams about her—hot, intimate dreams of the two of them tangled together? If he confessed that he woke up each morning as hard as a youth with plenty more hormones than sense? All he wanted was to cross the hall, rip open her door and climb into bed with her. He didn't care that she was Charlie's, didn't care that she was as unsuitable for Travis as he undoubtedly was for her, barely cared whether she would welcome him or scream the place down.

He ran a hand over his face. The whole time he'd been sitting here talking to her, all he could think about was moving closer, leaning over and burying his face against her softness. Of wrapping her legs around him and riding across the open land until they found a flat private spot where he could lay her down and climb on her like the animal her presence was turning him into.

To Travis's relief, one of the men shouted his name. He turned to see Adam waving his hat.

"I've got work to do," Travis said to Rory, as if she was the one who had called him away from it. "Don't stay out in the sun too long."

Before she could reply, he urged his mount forward, glad to put some distance between them before he lost it totally and hauled her onto the horse with him. Into his arms.

The next day, he still hadn't been able to shake the image of her, sitting atop the fence in the Stetson he'd brought her, blue eyes sparkling and wide, mobile mouth curved into a grin. When he walked through the door of the house, he was spoiling for a fight. What he saw when he got there gave him all the excuse he needed.

Chapter Seven

When Travis walked into the kitchen that evening, tired and sore from a long day in the saddle, the first thing he saw was Rory standing in the middle of the room with her suitcases at her feet.

Panic hit him with the full force of a sudden rain-squall. Dealing with fear the only way he knew how, he parked his fists on his hips and glared. ''What the hell are you up to?''

Her lower lip trembled and her lashes looked suspiciously moist, but her voice was as steady as a good pulling horse. ''It's time for me to leave.'' There were smudges beneath her eyes that hinted she'd slept no better than he had.

He'd spent the night in the bunkhouse, listening to the snores and restless shifting of the other men. This morning no one asked why he hadn't slept in his own bed. Cowboys didn't ask a lot of questions.

Now he leaned his hip against the counter and looked her over. She was wearing what she'd first arrived in, a gray tweed jacket and black jeans—and she had attitude wrapped around her like a fancy mink stole. Travis remembered how out of place he'd thought her when she came here.

She still didn't fit, but he cared less that she didn't. Hunger talking, not head, he reminded himself. Her purse was slung over her shoulder. She must have heard his truck drive up.

"Is this because of the other night?" he demanded.

She didn't pretend not to know what he meant. Her cheeks flamed. "No, of course not."

He wavered between relief and irritation at being dismissed out of hand.

"How are you getting to the airport?" he asked. "It's a long drive."

She glanced past him out the window. It was still light, but some clouds had blown in from the west. It would be dark soon, and they might have rain before tomorrow. He thought about simply refusing to make the drive.

"I called Adam," she said, surprising him. "He's taking me."

For some reason, Travis felt betrayed. She wasn't his, he reminded himself. He had no say in what she did.

"You heard from Charlie again," he guessed. "Now you're running out on him."

She bent her head, suddenly fascinated with the toes of her boots. "Yeah, he called the other night, after you left."

"And?" he prompted.

She shrugged and her chin went up into that familiar defiant gesture that tugged at him. Now he could see the tears shimmering in her eyes. "And I'm tired of waiting for him to come home."

Abandoning his stance by the counter, Travis shifted closer. He liked the fact that she nearly looked him in the eye, and he tried not to think about how they'd line up together, horizontal instead of vertical. "Why did you lie about coming here to marry him?"

Rory's mouth opened and shut, but no sound came out. She fiddled with her earring and looked away, as if searching for an answer on one of the cupboard doors. "I don't know," she whispered finally. "I'm sorry."

Travis remained silent as he studied her bent head. As usual, the color of her hair distracted him. Funny that he'd never once doubted its authenticity. It suited her so perfectly.

From the living room, the grandfather clock chimed the half hour.

"When's Adam coming?" Travis asked, feeling pressured.

"Soon." Rory's head lifted, and she hit him with the full force of her gaze. Her eyes were so dark, they were almost a violet blue. "How long have you known about Charlie and me?"

He wondered what else she'd remember from the conversation he'd overheard. "You were talking to Charlie on the phone a few days ago," he confessed. "I came back to get my gloves and I heard you."

She frowned, and then she shook her finger at him. "Why didn't you ask me about it then?" she scolded. "Too proud to admit you were eavesdropping?"

It was Travis's turn to blush. "It wasn't intentional." He had no inclination to let her turn it around, put him on the defensive. "Maybe I was giving you time to come clean on your own."

She whirled away, arms folded across her chest. "Oh, please." She paced the length of the kitchen. "You were waiting to trip me up, to hit me with it when I least suspected, like now."

Her accusation floored him. *He* wasn't the one in the wrong here. "If I'd wanted to do that, I'd have asked how a cold drink can got on my dresser."

For once, she was speechless.

"It doesn't matter now," he said, refusing to be distracted. "You came here under false pretenses. You said you were marrying my brother. I felt sorry for you, that's all."

"Is that why you made a move on me, out of pity?" She'd gotten her voice back and it rose sharply. Angry tears spilled down her cheeks.

His own anger was like a red haze in front of his eyes. For so long, he'd been proud of his control, of being in charge, his feelings firmly in check. This woman shot his control to hell. He glared.

Her nostrils were flared, her eyes glittered, and her chest heaved as if she'd been running. Her hands, he noticed, were balled into fists at her sides.

Suddenly, his anger was replaced by shame at what he'd said. It wasn't pity eating away at him, but desire. He wanted her. Was driven by it, tormented. And that wasn't her fault. *He* had kissed her.

"I didn't mean—" he began.

"No!" she cried. "No more feeling sorry for me."

Her gaze sliced through him like a filet knife, and then she turned and fled.

"Rory!" Travis followed her, slowly at first as he tried to figure out just where the conversation had gotten away from him. Then, when she pounded up the stairs, he heard a heart-wrenching sob. The sound galvanized him, and he took the stairs two at a time as a door slammed down the hall. Vaguely, he heard the sound of an engine from outside.

Hell. He went into his room and raised the window. Adam's truck was pulled up behind the house, and he was headed for the porch.

Travis raised the sash. "Adam!" he hollered.

His brother looked up. "Yeah?"

"Go home," Travis said.

"But Rory wants—" Adam began.

"I'll handle it. Go home."

Adam started to protest, but Travis ducked back inside and slammed the window. He waited, scarcely breathing, afraid Adam would walk right in and demand to know what was going on or that Rory would bolt down the stairs after him.

Her door remained firmly closed. After a few minutes, Adam's pickup left. Quietly, Travis went down the hall to Rory's room and listened. He didn't hear a sound. She must have heard him yelling at his brother. How did she feel about that?

Travis raised his fist to knock on her door, but then another sob, muffled this time, froze him in place. Heart thudding, he eased open the door.

She was sprawled on her stomach on the stripped mattress, her face hidden. The bedding was neatly folded on a nearby chair. Hell's bells, she really was planning to leave.

"Go away," she said in a tiny, waterlogged voice.

Travis's grip tightened on the knob. He could no more walk back out the door than he could cut off his own hand.

Rory felt the mattress sink under his weight, and she curled away in a miserable ball facing the far wall. Wonderful. Her mascara was a mess, her face red and blotchy. Her head ached dully. Instead of the image she'd planned to leave him with, one both dignified and, she hoped, reasonably attractive, he'd remember her with raccoon eyes and a snotty nose.

"Easy now," he coaxed, his voice deep and low. It sent shivers of longing through her. When had she realized she couldn't stay here with Charlie even if he did come back? She wasn't sure, only knew she'd never be able to think of Travis as her brother-in-law, or a brother in any sense of the word.

"What?" Her voice sounded sulky to her ears.

"Take this. Come on." Was that how he soothed a horse he wanted to break, a calf to be branded? Rory sighed and shifted so she could see him. He was holding out a tissue from the box on her nightstand like he'd hold out a lump of sugar.

Mumbling her thanks, she sat up and wiped her nose.

"Want me to get you some water?" he asked.

She shook her head, then wished she'd accepted so she'd have a moment in which to collect herself.

Travis didn't say anything else. The gray eyes she'd seen cold as ice or hard as steel were smoky, almost warm. His frown had softened, and his mouth quirked a little at the corners.

"I was never sorry for you," he confessed when the silence began to hum in her ears. "You're the toughest woman I know."

The compliment startled her into a laugh that came out watery. Her lips trembled. He handed her another tissue, and she blotted her eyes. "You're a better liar than I am," she told him.

"Wha—" Comprehension dawned. "I'm telling the truth. I don't know much about you, but what I do know is that you came out here into a totally different kind of life than you were used to and made a place for yourself. Charlie threw you a curve that would send another woman into full retreat, but instead you took over the cooking for a pack of hungry cowhands and did a damn good job of it. You moved in with a stranger, you did what you had to." He cleared his throat, sat back. "You've earned my respect and that of the other men."

His speech, one she suspected was a long one for him, made her start crying all over again. Respect! Oh, goody.

As she turned away, his hand closed over her shoulder. "What did I say?"

She dove back into the pillow, damp and cold from her tears.

"Is it Charlie?" he demanded. "Is he okay? What did he tell you?"

"He said he's coming home soon." Her wail was muffled.

Travis gave her shoulder a squeeze, and then he

gently urged her back up to face him. "That's good, isn't it?"

She sat up, shoulders drooping, and gave him a long, considering look. "I don't know anymore."

"If not to marry my brother, why did you come out here?" he asked.

How much could she tell him? "We'd been corresponding for months." She nibbled her lip. "I wanted to get away from New York for a while, and he invited me. We liked each other and we thought it might work."

His finger caught a last tear that trickled down her cheek. "What about your family? How do they feel about this?"

She thought of her former in-laws, all the family she had. She'd even given Daniel's mother the phone number here before she left New York. "My parents are dead," she told Travis. "I was ready for a new start."

"I'm sorry. Was it recent?"

She shook her head. "It was several years ago, not long after I was married."

"You mentioned an 'ex' before. I assume you're divorced?"

"Mm-hm."

"Charlie probably told you our father died, too," Travis said. "It was a heart attack, very sudden."

"Yes, he told me." And he'd told her their mother had left when they were small. They didn't know where she was or even if she was still alive. Rory couldn't imagine losing touch with your own children. She wondered how badly it had scarred them. Charlie hadn't said much about their father, just that he'd worked twenty hours a day. Reading between the lines, Rory had figured out that there hadn't been much time left over for his sons. "Losing your father so unexpectedly must have been very hard for you. I'm sorry."

He shrugged, obviously uncomfortable with the subject. "We had the ranch to run. There wasn't much time for grieving."

Rory reached out, put her hand over his. Looking down, he turned his over and linked his fingers with hers. With that simple touch, awareness throbbed between them.

"Rory?" Travis's voice was a rasp, her name a question. The very air around them pulsed with a life of its own. He seemed to be waiting for something. Her permission?

She pressed her hands to his chest and slid them up around his neck. Her fingers touched his bare, warm skin and she swallowed hard.

When she'd come out here, to Charlie, she'd been running. Running away. But now, for once in her life, she was going after what she wanted.

"Would you please kiss me again?" she asked.

Travis's eyes darkened with desire. Slowly, he reached out to touch her hair. Then he cupped her face with infinite tenderness.

"You and Charlie have no understanding, right?" he asked.

"Charlie and I are friends," she managed to say. That was the truth, as far as it went, she reasoned silently. "We made each other no promises, and I'm sorry I lied—"

He pressed a finger to her lips. "It doesn't matter."

It did matter, she mused as he leaned closer. But there would be time enough later to explain. It was the last coherent thought she had for quite a while.

If he never saw her again after tonight, Travis told himself as he pressed his lips against hers, he'd always remember her scent. It sank into him, sweet and seductive, filling his pores like a drug. And then there was her taste. Slowly, he slid his tongue over her lips, his whole body quickening when they parted for him. So easy. So inviting.

Her tongue curled along his, drew him in. He stretched out on the bed next to her and urged her closer. She melted against him, the tweed of her jacket scratchy on his cheek. He didn't dare take it off her and risk shattering the mood building between them. Instead, he pulled her silky top free of her jeans and slipped his hand under the hem, cupping her breast in its lacy covering. Her nipple peaked against his palm. His heart thundered in his chest, his blood draining so fast it left him light-headed.

Rory arched her back, murmuring softly, and pushed herself deeper into his hand. Her response threatened to shatter Travis's tenuous control. He'd been right; their bodies aligned perfectly. His hardness to her sweet, feminine softness. He tried to pull away, a last unselfish gesture, but she entwined her legs with his and her arms tightened around him.

"Don't go," she whispered.

He rose up on one elbow and studied her in the dimming light. "Are you sure?"

She buried her face into his shoulder and nodded, the trusting gesture all the encouragement he needed. He sat up and she cried out in disappointment.

"I'm just taking off my boots," he explained with a chuckle. "You might think about doing the same." He ended up helping her with them. Then he stripped off her socks and cupped her heel in his palm. Her foot was long and slim, her toes straight. There was a tiny blue butterfly tattooed on the arch and the nails were painted a cheeky pink. He wasn't sure he knew any other women with tattoos.

Before he could press a kiss to the butterfly, she slipped her foot from his grasp and peeled away her jacket. To him, the gesture was wildly erotic.

"Are you sure?" he repeated, heart thumping. "If I touch you again, I won't stop—not even for a herd of stampeding cattle."

In reply, she rose to her knees on the mattress and took his face in her hands. Her mouth was rosy from his kiss, her eyes filled with a woman's secrets. "I want you," she whispered. "Make love to me, please."

Rory thought he might start by undressing her or taking off his own clothes. Instead, he surprised her by drawing her down with him, cuddling her tenderly and kissing her with leisurely thoroughness. Her body began to hum. Then his lips traced the line of her throat while her senses filled with him, his heat, his scent, the feel of his touch, the sound of his voice as he murmured his approval, his breath when it caught.

Eventually, he did undress her. By the time he stripped away his own clothes to reveal a body that stole her breath, she was shaking with need, weeping with hunger. Damp with desire. When he finally entered her, slowly, steadily, they were both trembling with the force of their wanting.

His masculine strength overwhelmed her, but the tremor that ran through his big, powerful body at their joining captured her heart. They moved as one, and as she shattered around him, she heard his hoarse cry. Passion, possession and triumph.

It took a good long while for his breathing to get back to normal. With its return came a flood of common sense, too little and too late. At some point he had dragged one of the folded blankets over them. Rory lay in the crook of his arm, her eyes shut and the twin fans of her lashes edging the smudges beneath her eyes. Her hair was a wild tousle. He'd buried his face in it when he'd emptied himself into her—as irresponsibly and mindlessly as one of his own bulls.

Travis squeezed his eyes closed. Because of those irresponsible actions, he might have impregnated her. He'd certainly compromised her, taken advantage, whatever the modern terminology was. Never mind that couples fell into bed together all the time without a thought to the consequences. That wasn't his style. In some ways, he was a traditional man.

Either his restless shifting woke her or she hadn't been asleep. Her eyes fluttered open to reveal the still unexpected burst of navy blue that made his breath snag in his throat. Her lips, swollen from the pressure of his, curved in a soft smile. He wanted nothing more than to kiss her again, to begin again that glorious ascent that wiped out will and thought and, damn it, control from his brain as easily as wiping steam from a bathroom mirror.

Lightly Rory stroked the side of his face, the rasp

of her fingertips reminding him that his stubbly whiskers must have scraped her delicate skin like sandpaper. He should ask if he'd hurt her. Didn't think he wanted to hear the answer. Couldn't bear to.

Instead, he asked a question that common sense demanded.

"Um, are you on the Pill or anything?"

She shifted away from him, hurt in her eyes, and he knew he'd asked perhaps the worst possible thing he could have come up with.

She shook her head, and he could see the misty, romantic afterglow fade. "It's probably okay." Her voice was edged with doubt. She was telling him what she figured they both wanted to hear.

Travis swallowed. His timing was terrible, his handling of this situation abominable from start to finish. Still, his personal moral code refused to let him off the hook. She'd toss his offer back in his face, he was sure, but he had to ask the question that crowded his conscience, hummed inside him like music, speeded his pulse.

He took her cold hand in his and made himself look right into her eyes. "Rory, would you marry me?"

Had she heard right? Had Travis just proposed? She gave her head a hard shake, in case there was something wrong with her ears.

"Would you say that again?" she asked carefully.

His grave expression never faltered. His steady gaze didn't waver. "I'm asking you to marry me."

"That's what I thought you said. But why?"

He looked puzzled. "Why?" he echoed.

Suddenly conscious of her nudity beneath the

slightly scratchy blanket, she hitched it up higher under her chin and anchored the edges in place with her arms. When Daniel had proposed, they'd just finished dinner at a fancy restaurant. He'd presented her with a diamond ring, and they'd both had their clothes on.

Obviously, her demand to know why had caught Travis off guard.

"Just because we slept together and you didn't use protection, you're proposing?" she guessed. Was this, for pity's sake, what was meant by the Code of the West?

Travis colored. "What's wrong with that?"

There went the illusion that he'd fallen madly in love with her. As she had with him, she realized with a jolt of her heart. She did. She loved Travis Winchester.

Rory stared at him with a feeling not unlike dawning horror.

And he had handed her a proposal, albeit a reluctant one. He wasn't pretending anything else.

"What?" he demanded, getting to his feet as she struggled to deal with the sudden turn of events. While Rory stared, mesmerized by the sight of him, he scooped up his jeans and dragged them over his long muscular legs and his gloriously nude rear.

Wouldn't the denim chafe? she wondered distractedly, stifling a slightly hysterical giggle.

"Well?" he demanded after he'd fastened the fly.

She blinked. "Hmm?"

"You've been staring at me with the oddest expression," he complained, looking down at his bare torso as if he expected to find a horn growing from his stomach. "What's rattling around in your head?

Are you going to give me an answer? Do you need some time? I don't think—''

She glanced at her folded hands and then back at Travis. ''Yes,'' she said quietly, ''I'll marry you.''

A lesser woman might have been tempted to say that just to see his expression. He looked like a man who'd just been zapped by a stun gun.

Rory had never felt less like laughing. She considered telling him she loved him, but she suspected he wouldn't believe her. It was too soon. She'd have to show him, that was all there was to it. The circumstances surrounding their relationship might be less than ideal, but this was an opportunity she wasn't about to miss.

She would make him love her, she vowed silently, rashly. There was attraction between them, and passion. He was a man of the land, of the West, and already she liked what she saw of this country. They would find other common ground. People had started with less and been happy. Her feelings for him, though new, were strong. The risk to her heart, she realized, was high, but she was in too deep to walk away without trying.

In the last few weeks, she had lost a great deal, so many parts of her life until now, but she was determined not to lose Travis as well, not when she'd just found him.

He kept sneaking nervous little glances at her, as if he expected her to disappear. Perhaps he wished she would. Rory, on the other hand, admired the plain gold band he'd given her and remembered his possessive grip during the brief ceremony they had just been through.

"Are you hungry?" he asked, breaking the silence that had lasted since they left the small wedding chapel on the outskirts of Denver.

"No, are you?" she asked. They'd set out after breakfast and now it was midafternoon. He had offered to stop for lunch before they left Denver, but Rory had refused. Her stomach was still churning with emotion and she was afraid she'd disgrace herself.

He turned his head and his gaze touched her mouth. He had kissed her after they'd exchanged vows, a brief, polite kiss. Then something had kindled in his eyes and he'd pulled her into his arms to kiss her again. Only the minister's chuckle had pried them apart.

Heat ran up Rory's cheeks at the memory. That same look was in his eyes now. In the week since he had proposed, Travis had avoided her, leaving her to wonder if he was having second thoughts. For the last couple of days of the roundup they'd barely seen each other, and never alone. He had slept in the bunkhouse, while Rory continued to stay at the house and help Flynn with the meals. They'd heard nothing from Charlie, and she found herself forgetting all about him for long spans of time. Since she had made love with Travis, thoughts of him had taken over her life.

"You don't want to stop for anything?" he persisted, his attention riveted on the road ahead. One hand rested on the wheel, the gold band that matched her own gleaming brightly. When they'd stopped to buy rings on their way to the chapel this morning, she'd been inordinately pleased he was willing to wear one. Her one regret was that he had to pay for both.

She was sitting next to him in the truck. Now she put her hand on his thigh. "I didn't say that I didn't care to stop," she contradicted him. "Only that I'm not hungry."

He'd insisted they tell no one of their plans until they got back. Rory wondered if it was because he was afraid Adam might talk him out of it. She'd spent more than one night trying to decide what she would do if Travis changed his mind and making sure her own feelings for him were real and not the product of desperation.

At her words, his gaze snapped back to hers. He still wanted her, she told herself as she searched his face for clues to his feelings. That last kiss, the way he'd held her— She had passion, at least, to build on. Now his mouth curved into a grin at her reply. He didn't smile often, and this one had her reaching for her next breath.

"There's a motel down the road," he suggested, his voice deepening. For a moment his gaze roamed over her possessively. "It's nothing fancy."

Suddenly she realized he was as nervous as she, and as fearful of rejection. Deliberately, she leaned her breast against his arm and tightened her fingers on his thigh. Beneath her palm, his muscles leaped. Empowered by his response, she tipped back her head and studied him from beneath her lashes. Wait till he saw the nightie she'd impulsively stuck in her shoulder bag.

"We don't need fancy," she purred, lifting her

hand to trail one finger across his cheek. He was clean shaven, except for his mustache, and he looked terrific in a black-and-white checkered shirt, black Wranglers and a Western-cut gray suede jacket a couple of shades lighter than his Stetson.

Rory was wearing a soft green suit that had arrived with the rest of her boxes just days before. It had a fitted jacket and a short, straight skirt. Travis was tall enough for her to wear heels without worry, and she'd caught him sneaking glances at her legs in sheer silk more than once on their way to Denver. With the suit, she wore tiny emerald earrings that had been a graduation present from her parents and a gold lapel pin in the shape of a shamrock. Pinned to the collar of her jacket was the orchid corsage he'd bought her at a little shop next door to the jeweler's where they'd gotten their rings.

No, they might not have fancy, she thought, glancing again at her ring, but that didn't matter. What she wanted, what she was determined to have, was Travis's love.

In moments he pulled off the main road into a parking lot. The motel was pretty standard, two-storied with twin rows of doors, all numbered. The motel wasn't new, but it had been painted recently and there were a few green shrubs in a brick planter in front of the building. At this time of day, the lot was nearly empty except for several cars at the other side of the office.

Travis watched Rory look around. His palms were damp with anticipation and he could feel the tension curling in his stomach like a live snake. The last week had been hell. He'd thought of nothing but her, trying to figure out *why* she'd agreed to marry him. The days had dragged as he waited for Charlie to show up and claim her, or for her to turn tail and run back to New York. Now he could hardly believe they were married, they were here, and he was about to take her to a room and claim her.

Not if he didn't *get* a room, he realized.

"I'll be right back." Without looking at her, he bolted from the truck and headed for the office.

After he registered, they walked down to the end of the building. By the time he'd unlocked the door to their unit, Travis's nervousness had been replaced by a hunger that threatened to snap his control like a twig. Stepping back, he put a hand on Rory's arm when she would have preceded him through the doorway.

"Just a second, Mrs. Winchester." The words felt awkward on his tongue, but her smile was worth the effort. Suddenly, emotions he'd been struggling to suppress burst loose inside him. Bending down, he scooped her into his arms.

"Travis!" she gasped.

"What did you call me?" he teased.

Her cheeks bloomed with color, and her eyes danced with happiness he realized there was a good chance he'd put there. "Mr. Winchester," she whispered. "Husband."

His throat locked. Clearing it, he glanced around self-consciously and then he ducked inside. Kicking the door shut behind him, he set her down in the neat, generic motel room and wished they were in a honeymoon suite somewhere tropical and remote. Under the circumstances, a honeymoon had seemed inappropriate, but now he wasn't so sure.

Rory was looking up at him as though theirs was a love match. Could she really care for him? Naw, he realized with reluctance, she was just momentarily caught up in the spell. Women liked stuff like this, didn't they? Weddings, romance. The reality of their situation would come back soon enough.

Setting her down, he glanced around. There was a double bed with a flowered spread, matching curtains at the window, a television he didn't plan on watching, a closet and a door that must lead to the bathroom.

"This okay?" he asked without thinking. What if she said it wasn't?

She barely looked around. "Sure, it's fine. Um, excuse me." Quickly she crossed the room, clutching her shoulder bag, and disappeared through the door.

Now what? To combat the silence, he flipped on the television after all. A high school football game was playing on a cable channel, but he could barely concentrate. The minutes ticked by. He took off his jacket and put his hat on the dresser. Wondering if he should undress, he paced to the window, pulled the curtains shut and jumped before he realized it was his own reflection he saw in a mirror.

How long had it been since he'd taken a woman to a motel? Judging from the case of nerves plaguing him, too long. Over the sound of the game on the TV, he heard running water from the bathroom. At least she hadn't climbed out a window.

When the door opened, he was still smiling at the idea. When he saw Rory standing in the doorway wearing something long, lacy and sheer, his mouth went dry and his brain drained of coherent thought so quickly that his knees nearly buckled.

"Where did you get that?" he demanded.

Abruptly, her smile faded. "I brought it with me." Her tone was defensive, her chin thrust up in that gesture of independence he had come to recognize so well. Already he had some fence mending to do.

Quickly, he crossed the room to stand in front of her, absurdly glad he hadn't undressed and crawled into bed.

"You look lovely," he managed to say. "Breathtaking." It was hard to think when all he wanted to do was to ravish her. He struggled for more compliments, but they wouldn't come. He was too aware of his body's reaction to her.

Her expression had softened just a little. Raising her arms, she turned slowly. "You like it?"

The gown wasn't what had his blood bubbling in his veins, his breath snagging in his chest, his mind painfully blank, he realized. It was Rory. He wanted to say so, but the words were lost to him.

Travis did the only thing he could. He kissed her.

Rory stepped into his arms as if she belonged there. In moments, they were in bed, with nothing between them but the hunger that had grown hourly since they had come together that first sweet time. His hands swept over, his mouth claimed hers repeatedly. He tried to take it slow, savoring each tantalizing step, but she hurried him. Her touch was impatient, her tiny cries shedding his control. When he would have hesitated in one last effort at restraint, she crawled on top of him.

Everything in him reached for her. As she slid down over him, like a tight, wet fist, he thrust upward. Their hands linked, their bodies fused. Flesh melded with flesh, souls joined.

"Rory," he groaned as the red mist claimed him. "Wife."

Chapter Eight

Rory didn't want to open her eyes. Travis smelled of soap and piney aftershave. His breath danced across her bare skin; his heart beat steadily beneath her ear. Curled against his big, warm body, with his arms wrapped protectively around her, she could hold tight to the illusion that she was in bed with a husband who loved her as much as she did him.

As long as she kept her eyes closed, the possibility seemed very real. If she opened them, she might see merely sated lust on his rugged face—or worse.

Did he regret their hasty marriage? Was he feeling trapped by a proposal he'd believed himself duty-bound to make? And had she been wrong to take advantage of that sense of duty? Confused, she rolled over.

"Rory, are you awake?" Travis nibbled her bare

shoulder. His mustache tickled, his mouth was warm. Then she shivered as his tongue trailed over her sensitized skin.

"Mmm," she replied, snuggling closer with her eyes still tightly shut.

Gently, he palmed her bare breast as his arousal nudged her. Her breath quickened and she rubbed against him.

"Rory?" His arms tightened. Urgency threaded his voice. His thumb flicked over her nipple. He wanted her.

With a smile of pure pleasure, she shifted onto her back and stretched like a cat in the sun. His expression was watchful, his eyes dark with a passion he couldn't conceal. Her gaze wandered to his hard, clever mouth, and heat washed through her as she recalled what they had done in this bed.

Propping himself up on one elbow, Travis thumbed her nipple and bent his head. This time the loving was slow, thorough and exquisite. When they were finished, their bodies damp and drained, he shifted his weight to the side and cuddled her close. Then he lifted his head, glanced at the bedside clock and groaned softly.

"What's wrong?" she asked. Forming words was a struggle. She was limp and barely coherent. Travis had coaxed her over passion's highest peak more than once before allowing himself to join her in a final explosion of white-hot need.

Now he peeled back the sheet and dangled his feet over the side of the bed. His hair stuck out in spikes. As he ran a hand through the untidy strands, Rory watched the muscles of his back and shoulders flex.

"We have to get back to the ranch," he said, stretching. "I've got chores to do."

"We're on our honeymoon," she protested. The sheet had slid to her waist, but she was too content to care.

He turned to look at her, a lazy smile on his face. "Yeah, but no one else knows that." He bent his head and closed his lips over her nipple. Reaction shot through her. Just that easily, he reawakened the hunger she'd thought so thoroughly satisfied. She reached out for him, but he shifted away from her eager fingers.

Only when he stood up, gloriously nude, did she see that he was heavily aroused.

"I'll be right back." Expression rueful, he grabbed his Skivvies and headed for the bathroom.

He padded back out a few moments later. Still adjusting to the sudden intimacy between them, Rory scooped up her underwear and brushed past him, shielding her breasts with automatic modesty.

He put a detaining hand on her shoulder. "Let's go somewhere soon," he suggested. "A real honeymoon. Now that roundup's over, things will start slowing down. I could take a couple of weeks if we wanted."

Pleasure fanned over her like a sweet tropical breeze. "That would be fun." Two weeks with Travis all to herself!

Her enthusiasm seemed to encourage him. "Where would you like to go?" he asked eagerly. "As soon as Charlie gets back—" He stopped abruptly and his hand fell away from her shoulder. A muscle in his jaw twitched.

"When Charlie gets back...?" she prompted.

Travis studied her for a moment. "Is this going to be awkward for you?"

Rory smiled and moved closer, skimming a hand over his chest. Beneath her palm his heart skittered. She gave him a quick, firm kiss. "No, it's not a problem for me. How about you? He's your brother."

When Travis hesitated, head bowed, alarm shivered through her. "When we were in school he always got the girl I wanted," he began, rubbing the back of his neck.

"That's terrible," Rory murmured, instantly jealous.

Her immediate, unquestioning loyalty brought a warm glow to Travis. What did any of that matter anymore? Rory was his wife now. "He couldn't help it." Travis felt compelled to defend the brother he'd once resented so fiercely. "Charlie was outgoing, athletic, and he oozed charm like oil from a ruptured pipeline. Girls fell all over him." The memory was still a little painful. Once again Travis was the oversize, awkward, tongue-tied geek of his youth. "I had no idea how to talk to girls. To me they were as alien as little green men. When I'd finally work up the nerve to approach one, all she'd want to talk about was Charlie."

How frustrated he'd been in those days, wondering what was wrong with him. "He had no idea how much I resented him."

"You didn't tell him?" Rory asked.

"Are you kidding? He was my little brother. That made it doubly humiliating." Travis remembered his adolescent pain, the loneliness and the self-doubt as if it were yesterday. He'd never told anyone before, but Rory was easy to talk to and the words seemed to flow out of him.

Now she put her arms around his waist and rested her head against his shoulder. "I was taller than any of the boys in my grade," she confessed. "My chest was flat and my hair was orange. The curvy little blondes got the guys." She tipped back her head, eyes sparkling with shared laughter and remembered pain. "I think I can understand a little of what you went through."

A rush of warmth flowed through Travis, followed by a sense of peace and contentment. Crazy as it was, he'd done the right thing in marrying her.

The feeling continued as they drove back to the ranch, stopping for hamburgers on the way. Rory asked all about his childhood. He told her about his mother leaving when he was small and how devastated he'd been. He described his loneliness and the fear that his father would leave, as well.

Rory was a good listener. By the time they turned onto the ranch road, he realized he'd been doing most of the talking. Unusual for him.

"I'm sorry," he said sheepishly. "I don't usually rattle on like this. I've probably bored you crazy."

Cuddled next to him on the wide bench seat, Rory could feel him start to withdraw. "Don't say that." She gripped his arm. "I want to know everything about you."

He slowed the truck. There didn't appear to be anyone else around. "And I want to know all about you," he replied. "Like why you left New York and came out here. I think there's something you aren't telling me.''

Shaken by his perception, Rory glanced away. There would be time enough to relate the whole sad story, but she didn't want to think about it on their wedding day. ''It was time for a change, that's all,'' she said lightly.

For a moment, Travis held her gaze. Was that disappointment she saw in his eyes? Before she could decide, he turned his attention back to the road ahead.

''Any regrets?'' he asked quietly.

''Not so far.'' As soon as the words were out, Rory realized she was being too flip. As handsome and successful as Travis was, it was obvious to her that his childhood had been bleak and devoid of affection. He needed reassurance. She was just the one to give it to him.

''I'm glad we got married,'' she said. ''I love—'' she nearly blurted out her feelings for him, but then caution held them back. ''I love the ranch,'' she amended hastily. ''And Colorado. I have no regrets.''

''And Charlie?'' he probed. ''What about him?''

She tucked her hand through Travis's arm and smiled up at him flirtatiously. ''By the time he decides to come home, you and I will be a boring old married couple,'' she drawled, resting her head against his shoulder. ''Won't he be surprised?''

Travis insisted on carrying her over the threshold into the kitchen. Setting her down, he kissed her soundly. When he let her go, she noticed that the light on the answering machine was blinking.

''I told Adam we'd be gone for a while, but it

might be something important,'' he said when she pointed it out. Mildly curious, she waited while he pushed the button.

The first words from the tape jolted her complacency.

''Rory, I hope I'm not too late.'' She'd given Daniel's mother the phone number here, for emergencies, but she'd never expected him to call her. Not after the way they'd parted. It was as though his voice spoke to her from another lifetime.

''I can't believe you'd marry some cowboy you barely know just to get even with me.''

From the corner of her eye, she saw Travis stiffen.

''Your pride is hurt, that's all,'' Daniel continued in that all-knowing tone she detested. ''Fiona meant nothing to me, I swear.''

''They never do,'' Rory muttered.

''Come back so I can remind you how good it is between us.'' There was a pause on the machine and she glanced at Travis, face flaming. His arms were folded across his chest as he watched her with an unreadable expression.

''Forget this Western adventure of yours and come home,'' Daniel pleaded. His voice took on the underlying whine Rory hadn't noticed until after the divorce. ''You belong in the city, like me, not picking straw out of your hair while you wrestle some rodeo bum with a lump of chaw in his cheek. You'll be climbing the walls in a month.'' He sucked in an audible breath. ''I don't care if you're married or not. We can fix all that. Come on, Ro, give me another chance.''

Abruptly, the message ended. After the tape in the

machine rewound, the silence in the kitchen was deafening.

"Your boyfriend?" Travis asked. There was a chill in his voice.

"Ex-husband," she admitted. How she wished she'd explained everything when she'd had the chance. Daniel made the situation sound so different than it really was, as if she'd left in a snit because of him. She couldn't imagine him wanting her back. It must be dented male pride. He'd always had a lot of that.

"And you're still involved with him?"

"Not exactly," Rory hedged. She'd almost slept with him again, that was all. And she'd let him think Charlie wanted to marry her. "Daniel managed the diner where I was a cook, but we were divorced several years ago."

"Daniel?"

"Daniel Mancini," she replied.

Travis frowned. "That's right, you kept his name."

"My maiden name was Gumm. Wouldn't you?"

He didn't return her tentative smile. "And you kept working with him?"

"His family owned the diner. While we were married, they were my family, too." If only Travis would unbend a little, instead of standing so stiffly and so far away from her. The kitchen seemed to have expanded, opening a wide chasm between them.

"You had a fight?" he guessed.

"Well, yes." One evening Daniel had showed up at her apartment with a bottle of wine. She'd been lonely, he was familiar, and one thing had nearly led to another. When she'd come to her senses and asked him to leave, he was furious. In an attempt to make her jealous, he mentioned a waitress at the diner. His wandering eye had been one reason for their divorce.

That night Rory had been lonely, bored and a little tipsy. How could she explain to Travis that nearly succumbing to Daniel's sleazy brand of charm had appalled her? The whole episode was too humiliating.

Travis gestured to the answering machine. "You came out here to teach this guy a lesson? To show him you could marry someone else?"

She shook her head. Maybe her pride had let Daniel think that, but she would never have gotten married for such a lame reason. "I just wanted to get away."

"I think you wanted a husband and you didn't care who. When Charlie took off, I became a possibility. It really didn't matter, did it? You just needed a warm body to shove in this Daniel's face." His tone was condemning. "I wish you'd waited for my brother."

"No," Rory cried. "That's not true." He was turning things around, getting them all mixed up.

"When you came here to *visit* Charlie, did you have any intention of going back?" he asked. "Any intention at all?"

She hung her head. She couldn't deny it. What if he checked and found out there was no diner to go back to? What if he checked with her landlord? She'd given up her apartment and sold everything she hadn't shipped out here. How could she explain that, for once, she just hadn't thought beyond escape? "No," she admitted quietly. "I wasn't ever going back."

For a moment Travis looked out the kitchen window. "Like I said, anyone would do to make sure you could stay.'' Without glancing at her again, he left the room.

Trying to think what to do, Rory wandered into the living room and sank down on the couch. She wanted to run after him, but what could she say? He believed she'd been desperate, and she had. That much was true. Only not because of Daniel, at least not in the way Travis thought. First the diner had closed, and then she'd lost her savings in an investment scheme. Nearly sleeping with her ex had only been the last straw. She couldn't admit how foolish she'd been.

Perhaps what Travis needed was a little time to sort things out. She'd talk to him again later. To calm herself, she went into the kitchen and put the kettle on the stove. She was about to pour a cup of tea when she heard footsteps on the back porch.

She looked out the window and saw a shiny red truck parked outside, with fancy chrome wheels and wide tires. Before she could go to the door, it burst open and a tall cowboy wearing a black Stetson and carrying a leather duffel bag on one broad shoulder walked into the kitchen. His brown eyes crinkled at the corners, his smile a Winchester trademark she recognized easily.

''You've got to be Rory,'' he said as he set down the bag and removed his hat. ''Hi, I'm Charlie, the prodigal son.''

She stared, speechless, as he waited for her reaction. When she didn't move, his gaze dropped to her hand and his grin widened, revealing a matched set of dimples.

''Looks like congratulations are in order,'' he said.

Vaguely, Rory heard footsteps behind her. Before

she could speak, Travis walked into the room. He'd changed his clothes.

"Hi, bro." Charlie stuck out his hand. Ignoring it, Travis threw a punch that caught his brother square on the chin. Rory cried out as he crashed into the counter and nearly went down.

"Welcome home, *bro.*" Travis's temper might be red-hot, but his voice was as cold as the grave.

Staggering, Charlie gripped his jaw with one hand. As he worked it cautiously back and forth, his expression was unrepentent.

"I expected something like that from Rory, not you," he commented cheerfully.

"Yeah? Well, I'm the fool who married her in your place," Travis sneered. Rory cringed at his bitter tone. How quickly things changed.

Charlie's smile faded. "If you think I mind—" he began.

Travis's humorless laugh cut him off. "I don't give a damn if you mind or not." His gaze cut to Rory, whose cheeks were burning with humiliation and pain. The last thing she wanted was to make trouble between them. "And she didn't give a damn, either. She came out here to bag a cowboy, like a trophy elk, and that's just what she did. Lucky for you, *bro,* that you weren't here at the time."

Charlie glanced from Travis to Rory and back, clearly puzzled. "If that's the way you feel, why did you get hitched in the first place? Did someone hold a shotgun to your head?"

"Yeah, I held it to myself. At the time it seemed important." Travis looked at Rory, betrayal turning his eyes as hard as steel. "You can tell him if you want,'' he said. ''I don't even know anymore why we did.''

Heart breaking, she watched him stalk out of the room, grabbing his hat and coat as he left.

''Wow,'' Charlie said after the back door slammed shut behind him, ''I sure didn't plan on this.''

''On Travis and I getting married?'' she demanded.

''Naw. I kinda figured on that, if I stayed away long enough. I just thought you would have thawed him out a little by now, that's all.'' He touched his jaw gingerly. ''Travis hasn't hit me since we were in school,'' he mused. ''Still packs a hell of a wallop, though.''

''Wait a minute.'' Rory shook her head, totally confused. ''You weren't surprised that we got married?'' She felt as though, like Alice, she had just fallen down a rabbit hole. Nothing made any sense.

A wary expression came into Charlie's eyes as Rory studied him. His eyes were heavily lashed and topped by brows several shades darker than his hair. His nose was narrow and blade straight, set between cheekbones to die for, and his smile was devilishly sexy. It was easy to see why his flashy looks would turn female heads. Rory was surprised his appearance, even those killer dimples, didn't jolt her own pulse up by even one degree except in anger.

''I never meant for any of this to hurt you, I hope you believe me on that.'' His voice radiated sincerity he probably called up as easily as anyone else would order a pizza. She'd liked him a lot better before they'd met. ''All I wanted to do was to fix Travis up with a woman who'd appreciate him.''

She could scarcely believe what she was hearing. "Fix him up?" she echoed.

The dimples flashed, making Charlie look like a little boy who knew he'd been naughty but was sure he'd be forgiven. "Yeah. You and my brother, the loner. Worked like a charm."

"A *charm!*" She realized she was parroting him. "I'm married to a man who despises me, and you're patting yourself on the back for a plan well executed? I should slug you myself. You ought to be strung up. If lynching is good enough for horse thieves, it's way too good for you." Her voice had risen so that she was shouting.

"Now, wait a minute," Charlie cautioned, shaking his head. "I don't think that's true."

"What? That you should be strung up?"

"Actually, we don't do that anymore. What I meant was I don't think it's true that Travis despises you. His feelings are way more positive than that."

"On what brilliant basis did you reach that conclusion?" Why was she even talking to this man? Obviously, he was demented. Why hadn't this streak of insanity come out in his letters? "Why don't you think he hates me?"

Charlie touched his jaw again and flinched. "Because he's so damned mad."

Rory sent him a glare of disbelief, and then she sat down at the table and rested her head on her folded arms. "Wouldn't you be mad if your brother did this to you?"

"Well, maybe a little," Charlie conceded. "But I'm not Travis."

Rory didn't begin to understand what that was supposed to mean. Her head was whirling.

"You okay?" Charlie asked.

"Oh, sure." Normally she didn't care for sarcasm, but this man seemed to bring it out in her. She squeezed her eyes shut and stayed where she was.

After a moment of silence, she heard noises and lifted her head. Charlie was making coffee.

"Where did you go?" she asked curiously.

He got a mug from the cupboard. "Down to Baja. I hung out with a buddy, had a great time."

"Your brothers were worried about you."

Charlie drummed his fingers on the counter, waiting for the coffee to finish brewing. "That's the trouble with being the baby. No one thinks you can take care of yourself."

The complaint surprised Rory. In his letters, Charlie had sounded so upbeat, like a man without a care in the world. He'd been irresponsible in the extreme for disappearing the way he had, and his story about fixing her up with Travis sounded like bull. Before she could tell him that, Charlie filled his mug and brought it to the table.

"Now," he said as he turned one chair around and straddled it, "why don't you catch me up on your relationship with my brother."

She eyed him with suspicion. "Why should I?"

He shrugged easily. "Because I was right to get you two together, wasn't I? You're in love with him."

Rory's hand trembled violently and she nearly spilled her tea. "What makes you think that?"

He searched her face. "That's it, isn't it?"

It was her turn to hesitate. When she did, he leaned

forward to pat her hand. "Honey, I'm not the enemy, remember? No one knows Travis better than I do, not even Adam. When Travis and I were growing up, Adam was away at college, and then he had his hands full running the ranch after the old man died. Travis and I spent more time together than Siamese twins. Now, you gotta trust someone and it may as well be me."

Rory didn't know what to do. On the one hand, Charlie had manipulated her and Travis shamefully; on the other, he was all she had. Finally, toying with the handle of her teacup, she began to talk. She told him nearly everything except why Travis married her in the first place. That was too personal.

"You'll work things out," Charlie said, with far more confidence than she was able to muster. "I knew from your letters that you'd be perfect for each other."

Rory rolled her eyes. "In case you haven't noticed, I've been married less than twenty-four hours and my new husband has already walked out on me."

"He'll be back," Charlie replied, draining his coffee.

"What makes you think that?" Rory couldn't help but ask. Despite what Charlie had put her through, as a confidant he was easy to talk to. She'd already told him more than she'd intended.

"Travis will be back because I'm here," he drawled, dimples flashing outrageously. "My bro has been jealous of me since high school, and he won't leave me alone with his new wife for long."

"You knew about that?" Rory asked.

His grin widened. "Damn straight. I'm surprised,

though, that you did. Sounds like we've got even more reason to figure the two of you will work out whatever's stuck in his craw.''

Rory stared at her cooling tea. ''I wish I had your confidence,'' she muttered.

Charlie scraped back his chair and got to his feet. ''I'm going to get some clean laundry,'' he said as he opened the dishwasher and put his empty mug in the rack. ''I'll stay at Adam's for a few days.''

Rory wasn't sure she wanted to be alone. ''I thought you said Travis would come back because you're here with me.''

Charlie picked up the leather duffel bag he'd left sitting on the floor. ''Don't worry,'' he told her with a wink. ''I'll be around.'' He hefted the bag onto his shoulder. ''You two need some privacy to work things out.'' He studied her for a moment. ''Have you seen much of the ranch yet?'' he asked.

Rory blinked at the abrupt change of subject. ''No. I don't ride, and everyone's been pretty busy with the roundup.''

He ducked his head. ''Yeah, I know. It was a bad time for me to leave. When I went by Adam's, he was pretty steamed that I did. Just to make things interesting, why don't you come with me in the jeep tomorrow. I'll show you around.''

Rory had no doubt spending time with Charlie would only make Travis angrier. ''I don't think that's a very good idea,'' she said. ''But thanks for asking.''

''My brother can be awfully pigheaded,'' Charlie argued. ''You need to shake him up a little.''

''You don't think marrying me so suddenly has already shaken him up some?'' she demanded. ''Now he thinks I only did it to make my ex-husband jealous. How's he going to feel when he sees me spending time with you to make *him* jealous?''

''Let's find out,'' Charlie said with an unrepentant grin.

Rory shook her head. ''When he gets back, I'll talk to him. He and I have to work this out without any more manipulating by you.''

Charlie shrugged. ''Let's hope you're right. If you change your mind, I'm not that hard to find.'' He headed for the stairs. While he was packing, Rory stood at the window and watched for any sign of Travis's truck. The dirt road that ran by the house remained dishearteningly empty.

''Here's my pager number,'' Charlie said when he came back into the kitchen carrying the same duffel bag. ''If you need me, I'll get back to you as soon as I can.'' He must have realized what Rory was thinking when she glanced at his bag and frowned. ''Don't worry about my dirty clothes,'' he added. ''I'll wash them later.''

Rory trailed after him to the back door, beginning to understand what Travis meant about Charlie's charm. She should be mad as hell, and instead she almost hated to see him leave. ''You don't have to go because of me,'' she told his departing back. ''This is your home.''

''Adam will put me up,'' he replied. ''It will give me a chance to spend a little time with his daughter.''

''Sounds like Kim's had it tough, with her mom leaving and all,'' Rory commented. ''It doesn't sound as though they see each other very often.''

Charlie's smiled faded, and his eyes filled with

frustration. ''Christie's got other fish to fry. She never liked it here. She tried to get Adam to move to Denver, but he wouldn't consider it. What would he do there? The ranch is in his blood.'' Charlie grabbed his hat and set it on his head. ''You wrote that you thought you'd like it here,'' he continued. ''I know you haven't seen much of the ranch, but how do you feel about Colorado so far?''

The reply to that came easy. ''I love this country. It's so different from anything I've known before. There's so much space, and the air is so clean.''

Charlie pushed the back door open. ''Yeah,'' he agreed. ''I feel the same way. It's nice to travel, but it's nicer still to come back home.''

''You sure you don't want to stay here?'' Rory asked.

''I'll be fine at Adam's. You just put on something sexy. When Travis gets home, he won't even remember what he was upset about.'' He gave her another wink before he descended the porch steps. ''Trust me on that,'' he said, and then he got into his red truck. With one last wave, he headed down the road to Adam's house.

Travis didn't come back that night or the next. Rory spent all day alternating between giving the house a thorough cleaning and crossing to the kitchen window to look for his truck. Charlie called several times to check on her and to apologize yet again for messing up her life. He passed on the information that Travis had slept in the bunkhouse and he offered to come by, but she thought the sight of Charlie's red truck parked outside might be like waving a cape at a bull.

By the morning of the second day, Rory was climbing the walls. If she didn't get out, she'd go stir-crazy. Let Travis sulk and lick his wounds, she thought with a huff, she was married to him and planned to make the best of it.

Resolutely, she dialed Charlie's pager number. Within a half hour, he'd gotten back to her and persuaded her to take the jeep ride he'd previously offered.

"This is wonderful," she told him a little while later as they drove over a low rise and she spotted a small pond with ducks floating on its glassy surface. The day was cool, and the sky was nearly colorless. She'd bundled up, and the heater in the jeep warmed her feet and legs. After he'd asked how she was, Charlie had proved himself to be undemanding company. He had a bottomless bag of stories, and he wasn't above telling on himself to make her smile.

At first when they headed out, she'd been watching for Travis to appear. Then Charlie told her he and Adam had left for a nearby stock show that morning and would be gone most of the day. After that she relaxed, determined to put her new husband out of her mind. That she succeeded only for moments at a time wasn't anything she felt compelled to share.

Beside her in the jeep, Charlie leaned back and looked around. "This is part of the original acreage Dad started out with," he explained. "After our mother left, he worked twenty hours a day. He expanded and eventually bought out two of our neighbors. He got lucky. Beef prices held and land values skyrocketed.''

Rory glanced at a flock of birds flying overhead. ''You must have missed your mother, though.''

Charlie blew out a breath. ''I think in a way it was tougher on the other boys. I missed her at first, but eventually I just forgot a lot.''

''I'm sorry,'' she murmured, not sure what else to say. ''You never heard from her again?''

''Nope. But Dad built up one heck of an empire, I'll say that for him. Except for Adam's nemesis, the spread is pretty well laid out.''

''Adam's nemesis?'' she echoed. ''What's that?''

He pointed out past the pond. ''The Johnson land. Skinny little sliver, only about twenty acres, but it juts right into our property and nearly cuts off a third of it. There's only a thin neck connecting our main spread to one of the sections we added later. All the water at that end is his, too. Adam considers it his personal crusade to acquire that piece, but so far Johnson won't sell.''

''Well, perhaps someday he'll change his mind,'' Rory offered.

Charlie shrugged. ''He's pretty old, and he doesn't have any family. Anything could happen.''

After they'd driven for another hour, the wind picked up and Charlie insisted they head back. Rory had him drop her at the bunkhouse kitchen where she said hello to Flynn and offered to help with the cooking, but she was politely turned down. Instead, she went outside with Jane when the other woman took a smoke break. During the visit, Rory was careful to keep her left hand in her pocket. She had no idea whether Travis had told anyone, and she wasn't about to spill the beans if he hadn't.

When she finally walked up the road to the house, prepared to spend another night alone, his black pickup was parked outside and a light was on in the kitchen.

Taking a deep breath as tension, hope and excitement warred inside her, Rory headed for the porch.

Chapter Nine

Rory walked into the kitchen, disappointed to see that it was empty. Despite the way her new husband was acting, she missed his company. He'd been willing to marry her; surely she could break down the wall he'd erected after hearing Daniel's message on the answering machine. She hadn't come all this way to give up as soon as the road got a little rocky.

Maybe Travis had finally cooled off. The thought was enough to propel her up the stairs, quietly and quickly. Ignoring his closed door, she hurried to her bedroom. The moonlight streaming through the window was bright enough for her to see the room was empty.

Frustrated, Rory glanced back down the hall. If he had wanted company, wouldn't he have left his door open? What would he do if she climbed into bed with him?

The risk of rejection was too painful. Wrapping her arms around herself, Rory just hoped Travis was tossing and turning, as unable to sleep as she was bound to be.

By the time morning rolled around and Rory heard the sound of his shower rattling through the old pipes, she had a plan of sorts. She wasn't one to give up without a struggle; her father had always said her red hair was an outward manifestation of the stubborn streak she'd inherited from her mother.

When Travis walked in the kitchen a little while later, he was clearly surprised to see her sitting at the table in the robe he'd loaned her, sipping coffee.

"Good morning," she said, pretending the situation was entirely normal. The sight of him in work clothes, his broad chest covered by a Western-cut plaid shirt and his long legs sheathed in snug, faded jeans, made her breath catch in her throat. She could feel the heat of a blush warm her cheeks. Keeping her voice even was a struggle. "Did you sleep well?"

"Yeah, I guess." He didn't look rested. Warily, he watched her as he poured himself a mug of steaming coffee.

Rory resisted the urge to tug closed the deep vee neckline of her robe. When he didn't join her at the table as she had hoped he might, she got to her feet. Her knees trembled. Ruthlessly, she locked them steady.

"Would you like some breakfast?" she asked.

Leaning against the counter, he took a swallow of coffee. His strong fingers were wrapped around the mug, and a lock of his hair was already starting to fall forward, giving him a rakish look. "No, thanks. I'll eat at the bunkhouse. You didn't have to get up."

"I wanted to. Will you be home for supper?" she persisted. If he intended to continue avoiding her, he would have to spell it out.

She could almost sense the wheels spinning in his head as he tried to guess what she was up to. "I suppose I could," he said, surprising her. "If it isn't too much trouble for you."

"Of course it isn't," she said crisply. "You're my husband and I like to cook."

Looking uncomfortable, he glanced up at the clock. "I've got to go." He finished his coffee in two swigs and set the mug in the sink. His gaze flicked to Rory's as he circled around her and headed for the door.

"Is there a vehicle I could borrow today?" she asked before he escaped. "I really need to run a few errands in town." Now that the extra men were gone, Flynn didn't need her help with the meals and she had to find something to do or the tension between her and Travis would drive her crazy.

He hesitated and she held her breath, afraid he was about to refuse her request. Instead, he dug into his pocket and pulled out a set of keys. "Take my truck." When he handed them to her, his fingers brushed her palm, sending a jolt of reaction up her arm. His eyes narrowed slightly, and his mouth tightened at the corners.

"What will you drive?" she asked.

"I'll use one of the ranch jeeps." He hesitated. "Can you find your way to town alone? I could get someone to go with you."

Did he care about her, after all, or was it merely

an overworked sense of responsibility that prompted his offer? She wished she knew.

"You're welcome to come along," she suggested impulsively, risking rejection. Once she got him away from the ranch, perhaps she could persuade him to show her a little more of the country. They could stop somewhere to eat, take some time to talk.

He shook his head, shattering her pleasant little daydream. "Sorry, I've got a buyer coming out this morning to look at a couple of the horses."

Travis didn't look the least bit sorry, and he didn't suggest that she wait till another day. He was too eager to foist her off on someone else, but there wasn't anyone she wanted to spend time with but him.

"I'll be fine," she replied, laying the keys on the table. "Thanks, anyway."

"The ranch has accounts at most of the stores." He studied his boots with apparent interest. "Just tell them, uh, who you are. There shouldn't be any problem."

Was he embarrassed about their hasty marriage? Word was bound to get around eventually, especially if she started charging things in his name.

"That's okay," she replied. "I have some money."

He didn't argue.

"Have you told anyone about us yet?" she asked.

He held up his hand with its plain wedding band. "I haven't hidden anything."

It wasn't quite the response she'd hoped for. She would have liked to ask what the reaction had been, but the grandfather clock chimed the hour from the living room.

"I'm going to miss breakfast," Travis said. He warned her to be careful on the highway, and mentioned what time he thought he'd be back for supper. Then there was an awkward pause as they stood looking at each other. Rory wished he would kiss her goodbye. She debated initiating a kiss herself, but her nerves failed. Before she could think of anything more to say, he donned his hat and shrugged into his denim jacket.

"See you later," he said, and then he was gone.

Through the window Rory watched him walk down the road. She wished he'd turn and wave, but he didn't. Perhaps she should have offered to give him a lift in his truck, but if he saw how inexperienced she was with a stick shift, he could have changed his mind about letting her drive and she'd be stuck at the house.

After he disappeared and she realized she was still staring at the empty road, she went upstairs to shower and dress. A half hour later she was sitting behind the wheel of the pickup, thoroughly exasperated. Travis had made driving it look easy, but she must be doing something wrong. Every time she shifted into reverse, the engine bucked and died.

"Hi, darlin'. Need some help?"

Charlie's sudden appearance at her window startled her so badly she ground the key in the ignition. When she looked up, an angry retort on her tongue, his grin merely widened.

"Does my brother have any idea what you're doing to his transmission?"

"He's the one who gave me the keys," Rory replied defensively. "I'm going to Waterloo."

Charlie's eyebrows, so like Travis's, jerked upward. "You're driving?"

Rory thrust out her chin and wrapped her fingers around the steering wheel. "I'm planning to."

He opened the driver's door and she nearly fell out. "Move over, honeycake."

"What do you think you're doing?" she demanded, clutching the wheel even tighter.

"You can't go out in this thing alone. I'll take you to town."

Rory glanced around the yard, but there wasn't another soul in sight. "Don't you have work to do?" she asked.

He shrugged. "Things are slow. The ranch will run without me." He winked. "It has before. Do you want to go to town or not?"

How would Travis feel about her spending time with Charlie? Rory seriously doubted he'd be jealous; he didn't care enough for that.

Nibbling her lip, she decided to capitulate before she could change her mind. She undid her seat belt and slid across the bench seat. "If you're sure you can spare the time."

Charlie flashed his dimples. "I can always spare the time for a beautiful woman." As he climbed in beside her, his expression sobered. "Besides, I feel guilty about the situation you've gotten yourself into. I know it's all my fault."

It would be easy to let him take the blame, but Rory knew that wouldn't be entirely fair. "I don't remember seeing you at the wedding with a shotgun," she said as he slipped the truck into gear effortlessly and backed it around in a half circle.

"What do you mean?" he asked as they bounced down the dirt road. He drove faster than his brother.

"Travis and I were the ones who got married," she replied. "You had nothing to do with it."

Charlie looked annoyed as he shifted gears again. The transmission made a grinding noise. "If you say so."

The first thing Travis noticed when he walked in the kitchen late that afternoon was the heavenly aroma. Roast chicken, he guessed, mouth starting to water. It had been a long, hard day and he was starved.

Apparently Rory had made it to town and back okay. The truck was parked outside and none of the fenders bore any new dents he could see. Perhaps he should have gone with her, introduced her around, let her know her where things were. Not that Waterloo was so big a person needed a guided tour, but it might have been nice to show her off.

Would people wish them well or laugh behind his back at his foolishness in taking an outsider for a wife? Another Winchester making the same mistake, they'd say. Didn't those boys ever learn?

He was about to call out that he was home when he noticed the kitchen table. It was covered with a blue cloth. In the center sat a vase of yellow carnations, a white sugar bowl and matching salt and pepper shakers. The table was set for two.

Before he could look around to see what else she might have done, Rory walked into the room. She was wearing a blue sweater and jeans, with a flowered apron tied around her narrow waist. She looked good, the kind of woman a man liked coming home to. Not city, not country, just pretty.

His heart melted a little.

"Hi," she said softly. Her lips curved into a smile he was tempted to taste, just to see if it was as sweet as it looked. Realizing the direction his thoughts were taking, Travis returned her greeting curtly.

"Dinner will be ready as soon as I make the gravy," she said, apparently unfazed by his surliness. "Why don't you wash up." She busied herself at the stove, her movements capable and unhurried.

His stomach emitted a growl of anticipation. Hastily, he went upstairs. There, to his surprise, he noticed that the bed he'd haphazardly pulled together that morning was neatly made. In the bathroom, the mat he'd left in a heap on the floor had been straightened. A fresh bar of soap in a new green dish sat next to the gleaming sink. The old-fashioned chrome faucets sparkled, as did the mirror.

Suspiciously he looked around, but could see no further evidence of Rory's touch, not even another soda can on his dresser. As he washed up, he debated saying something about her coming into his room, and then he realized the absurdity of it.

For better or worse, they were married. He grabbed a fresh towel, one he didn't remember seeing before. It was fluffy and had a pleasant smell.

All the way back down the stairs, he wondered what she was up to.

"I've invited Adam and Kim to dinner tomorrow evening," Rory said when they sat down to eat. "I hope that's okay with you.'' Meticulously, she unfolded her napkin and spread it on her lap.

Travis wanted to remark that it was a little late to think about what he wanted, but he glanced down at his heaping plate and prudently held his tongue. ''Sure,'' he mumbled instead, after he'd bitten into a warm corn muffin.

Rory seemed to be waiting for something, but when he dug into the mashed potatoes and gravy, she began nibbling at her own dinner. Just before she bent her head, he saw the sparkle in her eyes go dim. The bite of potato that had looked so tempting turned to sawdust on his tongue.

''It's good,'' he said after he'd managed to swallow.

Her head popped up and a smile blazed across her face. His gut tightened in reaction. ''I'm glad you like it.'' The light was back in her eyes and Travis realized his approval had put it there.

He stared hard at the white meat he was cutting. ''The table looks nice, too.''

''You don't mind that I did a few things?'' she asked. Her voice sounded genuinely anxious.

Travis stopped filling his face long enough to glance up again. She was watching him intently. ''Maybe the place needed a woman's touch,'' he admitted. ''No one's done anything around here in a long time.'' No one had cared what the place looked like, as long as it was functional, not since his mother left so many years before. Even the kitchen remodeling had been for practical purposes, not aesthetic ones.

To his horror, Rory's eyes glittered suspiciously.

Before he could get a good look, she leaped from the table.

"I forgot the cranberry relish," she mumbled.

Unsure what to do, Travis started eating again. When she sat back down, he noticed her cheeks were flushed with rosy color and she kept her eyes downcast.

"I didn't marry you to spite Daniel," she blurted. "I wouldn't do that. The phone message you heard was him doing his best to get the last word, that's all."

Chewing thoughtfully, Travis mulled over what she'd said. Then why had she married him?

"Aren't you going to say anything?" she demanded.

"Didn't sound like a question," he replied.

She made a sound of disgust in her throat.

"Maybe I shouldn't have walked out the way I did," he conceded, surprising himself. Before Rory could reply, he ducked his head and forked up another mouthful of potato. She must have realized how uncomfortable the whole subject made him, because she didn't say anything else.

By the time the fierce edge of his appetite had been appeased by a generous second helping, the silence between them began to feel strained. "How was your trip to town?" he asked. "Did you have any trouble?" How many people had she told they were married?

"No trouble at all," she replied with a bright smile. "Charlie went with me and showed me around."

Travis's fork clattered against his plate as a wave of jealousy tore through him. It turned the pleasantly full feeling in his belly to a hard, burning lump. "I thought you were going alone," he accused.

"If you remember, I did invite you first," she replied.

Temper flaring, Travis shoved aside his half-full plate. "And when I turned you down, you went to the next name on the list?" He knew he was being unfair, but old habits were hard to overcome, and losing out to his charming younger brother was obviously still a sore spot.

Losing what? a little voice in his head taunted. A wife who'd come here, despite her protestations of innocence, to punish one man, to marry another and ended up settling for a third? In the midst of pushing back his chair, Travis hesitated. Then a new wave of anger washed over him. He'd be double damned if he'd let feelings he couldn't understand tie him into knots.

"I didn't go looking for Charlie this morning," she protested. "He came by and offered to go with me."

Travis got to his feet, stomach churning with frustration. He needed some space. He needed to think.

"Where are you going?" Rory asked. "You haven't finished eating."

He glanced down at his plate, surprised to see she was right. "I've lost my appetite." He knew he was acting childishly, but he was unable to stop himself. "Excuse me." The words were automatic. His father had demanded good manners.

Without looking at her again, he headed for the living room and the television he hardly ever watched. Mindlessly flipping through the channels, he tried with little success to focus on the oversize screen and to shut out the sounds of banging pots and pans from the kitchen. He had no idea why he felt so guilty when he was the one who'd been wronged.

"What's your favorite subject in school?" Rory asked Kim as Adam's daughter helped her dish up dinner the following evening. The two men had gone immediately to the living room, where they were discussing something to do with wintering the cattle.

Kim had long, dark hair that curved under at the ends and was anchored at the sides with green barrettes that matched her eyes. She was wearing blue jeans and a gold sweater that turned her skin a little sallow. In the act of putting dinner plates around the table, she hesitated.

"I like English the best, I guess. And history." She smiled shyly. "You sure have pretty hair."

Rory rolled her eyes. "I didn't think so when I was your age. I was the only redhead in my class and the other kids teased me a lot. But thank you for saying so."

Ducking her head, Kim finished setting the table. She was a sweet girl, painfully eager to please. She must miss her mother terribly. Charlie had mentioned in his letters that Adam's ex-wife seldom saw her daughter, and Rory wondered how any woman could abandon her own child. It was obvious that Travis's experience had scarred him and made him wary of emotional commitments. It must have affected all three of them, though perhaps in different ways.

Rory's heart ached for the vulnerable little boy Travis would have been, waiting for his mother to come back. Why had she left and what ever became of her that she never returned or contacted her children again? Did she care that she had a grandchild or did she even know? Maybe someday Rory would ask Travis if he had any idea.

She finished slicing the roast and set the platter on the table. ''Why don't you get the salad out of the fridge and call the men,'' she suggested to Kim as Rory removed the pan of scalloped potatoes from the oven. ''It's time to eat.''

She'd been worried that dinner might be awkward, what with the continued strain between her and Travis. Instead of the long, painful silences she'd envisioned, conversation flowed with ease. Adam described the trip to Disney World he and Kim had taken that last spring and plied Rory with questions about New York. Kim talked about the rabbits she was raising for her current 4-H project, and even Travis contributed a couple of entertaining stories about the recent roundup.

''I think dinner was a hit,'' Rory commented to him after Adam had finally mentioned school in the morning and herded out a reluctant Kim, who'd given Rory a hug at the door. To her surprise, Travis had remained in the kitchen to help her clean up instead of retreating to the television or his bedroom as she'd expected.

He looked up from the counter he was wiping. ''Yeah, the evening went pretty well.''

''Adam had two helpings of dessert,'' she continued, reluctant to let the conversation die. ''Is chocolate a particular favorite of his?''

Travis's expression softened. ''Anything sweet is a favorite of Adam's. When we were little he was always getting in trouble for stealing candy or cookies from the kitchen without permission.'' Travis frowned, eyes blank, and Rory wondered what he was thinking.

''A little boy raiding the cookie jar sounds pretty normal to me,'' she ventured. Her own mother had baked every week, filling the pumpkin-shaped jar in their cozy kitchen. It had never been off-limits.

''It wasn't normal around here. We got a whipping for things like that. The old man didn't believe in sparing the rod.'' Travis's voice was harsh and Rory shuddered.

''That's terrible,'' she exclaimed. His childhood sounded like a perfectly miserable experience, his father strict and cold. After their mother left, Travis and his brothers would have needed even more love and affection, not regimen and punishments.

''He had a ranch to run,'' Travis replied defensively. ''He wanted us to be tough enough to take it over someday. None of us knew we'd have so little warning, though, when the time actually came.''

Rory turned to face him, hands in her pockets. ''He died suddenly?''

''Heart attack. He was already gone when they found him. Adam was in college. Charlie and I were still in high school.'' He rubbed a hand over his face and sighed. ''Adam came home. I still don't know how he kept the place together those first few years.''

Rory wondered if Travis would bolt if she suggested they sit at the table with some coffee. She decided not to risk it. ''You and Charlie must have been a big help,'' she pointed out instead.

''Yeah, that first summer was unreal. I don't think

any of us slept more than three hours a night, but Adam worked like a demon.'' Travis leaned past her to put the cloth he'd been using in the sink. She shifted slightly, drawn to him like a metal filing to a magnet. He froze, arm still outstretched. His stare was fixed on her mouth. For a timeless moment, neither moved.

Abruptly, he straightened away from her. ''Tomorrow comes early,'' he said gruffly. ''Thanks for supper. I'm turning in.''

Quelling her disappointment, Rory kept her tone light when she bade him good-night. If the huskiness in his voice was any indication, he wasn't completely immune to her nearness. For now that would have to be enough.

She was driving him crazy. Unless he rode clear out to one of the far pastures, he saw her everywhere. When he was home she was underfoot, fixing his meals, putting away his laundry, doing the little feminine things around the house he hadn't even known he was missing. When he rode fence or looked after stock, he'd see her in a jeep with Charlie or Adam. She'd wave and her laughter would drift on the air like perfume. What did his brothers say that made her laugh?

Barney was teaching her to ride; Jane helped her sew curtains for the kitchen and bullied Travis into noticing after they were hung. He didn't know Rory had needed teaching how to drive a stick shift until Charlie mentioned he'd done it. When the family went to church on Sundays, Travis had no choice but to take Rory along. She sat in the pew next to him, and they listened to Charlie sing in the choir.

Apparently she hadn't told anyone in town about their wedding, but word was getting around. The first Sunday they'd gone to church, Travis had been forced to introduce her to the pastor. Phoebe Pennyweather had overheard; from there the news had spread like a prairie fire in a stiff wind.

They'd gotten invitations to two gatherings at other ranches. The first Travis had managed to dodge; the second, a neighbor's eightieth birthday party, had been impossible to miss. Adam, Kim and Charlie, with a date from town, had been there, too.

On the way back to the ranch that night, Rory sat beside Travis on the wide bench seat in compatible silence. She'd been quiet but friendly at the party, drawing out people by listening to them and freely answering questions about New York when she was asked without being too pushy. The Malone girl who worked in town had cornered her for quite a bit, peppering her with questions until Travis thought to rescue her.

Ranchers and their wives were a conservative group, but he could tell they took to her. There wasn't much not to like, despite her flashy appearance. He'd even found himself proud when the other men sneaked looks at her dressed in a fuzzy sweater and snug-fitting cords.

Now she was bundled into the heavy parka he'd insisted she buy in town. Around them, the night was cold and clear. Surprising himself, he reached for her gloved hand and held it loosely. "Did you have a good time?" Would she admit she found his friends provincial, the conservation boring, the music and refreshments hopelessly out of fashion? She must realize that, despite tonight's success, she had little in common with any of the locals.

She squeezed his hand. "Mae Sweeney's amazing," she said. "Imagine being born on a piece of land and living your whole life there."

"It must seem like a waste to you. She hasn't been anywhere."

Rory turned to look at his profile. "Shc's raised eight children and she ran the place practically singlehandedly after her husband was killed, even though she has diabetes and trouble with her feet," she said. "She still has a big garden every year, and she showed me all the food she's put up. Rows of jars in a little room her husband built on. Plus she's working on a lovely quilt for a raffle at church. I admire her tremendously."

Travis had known the woman all his life, but Rory had learned more about her in one evening than he had in thirty years. Adam's wife had never mingled with the local women, never made friends at church. She complained that all they talked about was cooking, babies and weather.

"When the snow comes, we'll be isolated for weeks at a time," he warned Rory. "The phone lines go down and the power fails. You'll get bored. The house will close in on you."

Her chin went up. "I'm never bored."

His smile was without humor. "We'll see," he said as he parked the truck. He hadn't meant the comment as a challenge, but from her expression, he guessed she took it as one.

When he helped her down from the truck, the night air stung his cheeks and turned his breath to smoke. The moon was high and bright, lighting her face as she looked up at him. Her eyes were shadowed and hard to read.

"I'm not leaving," she said, surprising him. "You might as well get used to it."

Travis wanted to believe, but caution and common sense ruled. All he could do was to make damned sure she wasn't taking a piece of him with her if she did go. He'd seen Adam bleed. "Tell me that when you've got a Colorado winter under your belt," he replied.

She chuckled low in her throat and his breath caught. "I will," she purred, stroking his cheek with her gloved hand, "and it won't be on a postcard. I'll be right in your face when I say it."

From the way he reared back from her touch, Rory could tell he wasn't buying her words. She had to find some way to convince him she'd stick, and she didn't intend waiting until spring to do it.

"It's cold out here." She'd said enough for him to chew on for a while. "Let's go in."

When she turned away, he hooked his hand through her arm. "Greenhorn," he taunted softly, surprising her. "If you think it's cold out now, wait a month."

She searched his face in the moonlight. His expression had changed, his eyes turning black and hot, and a smile played at the corners of his mouth. While she studied him, he dipped his head.

His lips were cool, but they heated quickly against hers. Surprise parted her lips and he took advantage, deepening the kiss as his arms tightened around her.

Despite their bulky clothes, Rory could feel his strength and the tension humming through him. His hips bumped hers, his arousal straining through layers of denim and corduroy. Her knees turned to jelly and her legs quivered. With a will of their own, her hands slid down the front of his jacket and burrowed around his waist.

He changed the angle of his mouth on hers and her head swam. His hand slipped under her jacket and his fingers curled over her breast. Her nipple beaded beneath her sweater, and she pressed herself against his hand as the memory of his lovemaking heated her blood.

He broke off the kiss and buried his face in her hair, his breath whispering against her cheek. His groan was as sweet as any angel's chorus, his arms a magic circle around her.

"Let's go inside," she gasped. Surely he'd come to bed with her. They were married; he wanted her. The proof was pressed against her own liquid heat.

He didn't answer, but she felt him stiffen, start to withdraw. She pressed her lips to his cheek. Despite the cold, his skin was hot. Her tongue found his ear, traced its shape as he shuddered.

"Rory," he croaked. A plea to stop or go on?

Encouraged, she grasped his hand, tugged him toward the steps. In the ghostly moonlight, his face was all sharp angles and hollows. He took one step and then another. His arm curved around her waist, holding her close.

Any further protest he might have made was lost in another kiss. This time, when they broke apart, he was the one urging her inside. In the kitchen, he peeled off both their coats and thrust them at hooks. His fell to the floor and he scooped it back up, his movements jerky and impatient. His eyes, when he turned, were hooded, his cheeks streaked with color. Rory was trembling, her senses clamoring for his touch, her being starved for his possession.

"It will be okay," he gasped as he all but dragged her toward the stairs.

"Of course it will," she agreed, having no idea what he meant. Was he worried about pleasing her?

"I'll protect you. I bought condoms."

She'd given no thought to birth control. Now she refused to let the practicality of his remark destroy all that was building between them. Neither did she know how to respond. All she could think of was him, and them, and fusing bodies and minds and emotions. She hesitated at the door to his room, but he urged her down the hallway to her own room and followed her inside. When his fingers closed on the hem of her sweater and he tugged it over her head, she forgot all about where they were or why. It was only later, sated and sleepy, when she saw him gathering up his clothes, that she realized why he'd come to *her* room.

So he could leave.

"Stay," she murmured, stroking a hand up his bare thigh. The wiry hairs tickled her palm pleasantly and his muscles quivered.

He leaned over and kissed her, but she could sense his withdrawal and her heart ached. "You'll rest better alone," he said.

Suddenly angry, she bolted upright, holding the sheet against her breasts like a shield. "No, you'll rest better alone,'' she told him. ''I hope your bed is ice-cold and lonely as hell.''

She felt his gaze in the darkness. His hand touched her hair, a caress so featherlight she almost missed it, and then the mattress shifted with his weight. She thought she heard him mutter ''What else is new,'' but she wasn't sure. Her bedroom door closed softly behind him, the faint snick as final as a gunshot, and then she pressed her face to her pillow as the tears of frustration took over.

From the other side of her closed door, Travis thought he heard a sob, so faint he wasn't sure if his ears were deceiving him. His hand tightened on the knob.

He could still go back, could still spend the night in her arms. Ears straining for some sound, fists clenched at his sides, he struggled for control. Several minutes went by before he managed the first steps away from her, several minutes in which he called himself every kind of fool. Even when he was settled into his own bed, as cold and lonely as Rory had wished it to be, he still wasn't sure if he'd passed the test or failed it. Or why he'd even tried.

Chapter Ten

"How's it going?" Charlie asked when Travis walked into the bunkhouse kitchen and poured himself a cup of coffee. Charlie was sitting at the table with a sandwich. His feet were propped up on a chair. He'd never been the sort to hold a grudge. Travis, on the other hand, wasn't ready to make peace, not when Charlie spent so much time entertaining his wife.

Travis had shed his slicker in the hallway and left a puddle there, but the hard rain had also managed to find and soak his shirt collar, cuffs and the legs of his jeans below his knees. The dirt roads had turned greasy in the storm, and his arms and shoulders ached from his efforts to keep his pickup from bogging down.

"How's what going?" he asked defensively. What if Rory decided she'd married the wrong brother?

Charlie finished the sandwich he'd been eating and got to his feet, but he kept his distance. ''How's life treating you? That's all I meant.''

Travis relaxed a little. ''Okay, I guess.'' He set his mug down on the table, but he remained standing so he wouldn't have to look up at Charlie.

''How's that pretty new bride of yours?'' Charlie persisted with a grin that Travis was suddenly and keenly tempted to wipe off with his fist. He wasn't usually a violent man, but Charlie seemed bent on goading him.

''You should know better than me how she is,'' Travis growled. ''You spend more time with her.'' Ever since that last night in Rory's bed, Travis had been climbing the walls, trying to stay away from her. She made it damn difficult, batting her eyes at him, smiling flirtatiously. Accidentally touching him or brushing up against him. When he was around her, he was as hard as a kid with a dog-eared *National Geographic.*

Why didn't he just move her stuff into his room and be done with it? He doubted she'd object. He watched her carefully for signs of boredom, but she seemed content to fix up the house with little feminine touches he secretly enjoyed and to hum while she puttered in the kitchen. Maybe he was plain crazy for being so wary. He should take what she offered and enjoy it.

Charlie's gaze had sharpened imperceptibly. ''If you don't like Rory spending time with me, find some for her yourself. She's your bride, big brother, not mine.'' His tone was unusually sharp.

"Only because you got cold feet and took off like a yellow coward."

The only explanation Charlie had given for his disappearance was that he'd met up with a friend down in Baja. Travis hadn't pressed; perhaps he should have. Now Charlie threw back his head and laughed at the taunt. Still grinning, he clapped Travis on the back. "Admit it," he crowed. "You're jealous."

He looked way too smug to suit Travis, who struggled to keep his voice even. "Jealous?" he echoed. "You never even met her before you split."

"Good thing, too," Charlie replied, taking a toothpick from his shirt pocket and tucking it into the corner of his mouth.

"What's that supposed to mean?" Travis demanded. Surely Charlie wouldn't go after his own brother's wife?

Charlie glanced down at the fists Travis hadn't even realized he'd formed. The toothpick danced in Charlie's mouth. "If I'd have seen her first, I might not have left," he taunted. "What all did you expect I meant, bro?"

When Travis didn't immediately reply, he smirked again and headed for the door, whistling a hymn Travis recognized from the church service just last week. "Better watch your back," Charlie called over his shoulder. "Not every guy who likes redheads feels the way I do about married women."

Travis was halfway around the table when he managed to get himself back under control. Charlie loved to bait him, but his jibes usually rolled off Travis's back like water off an oilskin tarp. Suddenly the urge to deck his mouthy little brother was getting to be habit—one Travis didn't like at all.

"You should join the choir at church," Charlie told Rory. "I'm serious. You've got a great voice, and we harmonize as if we'd grown up singing together."

Blushing, Rory looked away. They were on horseback. Barney had told her the day before that she needed practice more than lessons and Charlie overheard. He'd insisted they ride out today while the sky was clear. He often sang snatches of songs when they were together, and this time she had timidly joined in. Instead of being annoyed, Charlie had smiled his encouragement and immediately followed the first song with another she knew.

"I've never sung in public," she admitted. "I'm a shower crooner."

"Could have fooled me. Since you're married to my brother, I won't make the obvious comeback." Charlie studied her for a moment while the horses picked their way down a shallow ravine. Officially, they were looking for strays, but they hadn't seen one cow.

"I've got an idea," he said when they reached the bottom. "Why don't you and I work up a duet for the fall program? The director asked me about doing a number, but it's no fun performing by myself."

His suggestion astonished Rory, who'd always considered her voice mediocre. "You're kidding, right?"

Charlie shook his head. "I'm dead serious," he said, grinning. "Two reasons."

"You've lost your mind and you're a glutton for punishment?" she teased. Since they'd been spending time together, she and Charlie had managed to recapture the easy footing they'd shared as pen pals. Not that she'd forgiven him for all his manipulating; she hadn't. But she was lonely and Travis was always busy. Maybe being a friend was Charlie's way of trying to make up for all his meddling.

Now he laughed at her remark. "That's probably true enough," he said, "but not where you're concerned. Seriously, our voices seem to complement each other's really well."

Rory could feel her blush spreading. "And the other reason?" she asked.

"It would drive Travis crazy."

It was Rory's turn to laugh, at least with disbelief. "I don't think so."

Charlie reined in his horse and put a hand over hers. "He's eaten up with jealousy."

Rory was tired of pretending. "You're wrong. Travis doesn't care—" Sudden tears filled her eyes and she turned away. The truth was too painful to admit, even to Charlie.

"Rory," he said quietly, waiting until she looked at him again. "Will you trust me on this? I know my brother. There are reasons for his caution, but he cares for you more than he's admitting, even to himself."

A little spurt of hope rose in her, refusing to be squashed. "You really think so?"

"You love him, don't you?"

What an odd question to be asking a newlywed. "How could you tell?"

"When you're around him, you glow," he said simply. "If a woman ever looks at me the way you look at Travis, I think I'll just have to marry her, too.''

She didn't know how to reply. ''You're a good man,'' she began.

''This isn't about me.'' His voice was unusually sharp. A few feet away, a rabbit bolted from the bushes. Charlie's horse shied, and his head went down as if he meant to buck. By the time Charlie had regained control, he was his usual smiling self. ''Let's turn the screws a little and see what happens,'' he suggested.

Rory searched his face. The last thing she wanted was to hurt Travis or upset him, but the situation between them wasn't getting any better. ''Okay,'' she said breathlessly. ''I hope you know what you're doing.''

Late that afternoon, as she waited for Travis to come home so she could put supper on the table, Rory was still trying to figure out how Charlie had managed to extract her promise to sing with him if the choir director gave his okay. What had she been thinking? It was Travis she wanted. Hadn't she had enough of Charlie's crazy schemes?

To be perfectly honest, the minute he'd mentioned Travis and jealousy in the same sentence, she'd jumped at the chance to see if it was true. Part of her, a big part, didn't buy the idea, but she was hungry for any sign that Travis cared about her. It wasn't only her husband she'd fallen for, but the whole ranching life-style. She liked the people she'd met, their fierce independence and their dependence on one another. Despite the fact that Rory was a city girl born and bred, she felt as though she'd found her calling as a rancher's wife. No one, not even the rancher in question, was taking that from her, she vowed as she sliced pickles ruthlessly. All she needed to be happy was knowing her husband cared.

"You're frowning," Travis said from behind her, startling her so violently that she nearly cut her finger. He always managed to sneak up on her. "Something wrong?"

As usual the sight of him sent Rory's heart rate soaring. She wanted to throw her arms around him and greet him like a proper wife. "I've agreed to sing a duet with Charlie for the fall pageant at church," she blurted instead. "He has to clear it with the choir director, but I'm already having second thoughts."

"I didn't even know you could sing." Travis's scowl was gratifyingly fierce.

Rory wiped her hands on her apron. "I'm not sure that I can."

He crossed his arms over his chest. "Then why did you agree?" he asked in a practical tone.

Rory would have given a lot to know what was going on behind his steady gaze. It was impossible to tell what he was thinking. "If you don't want me to do it, I'll tell him I can't," she said, already hoping for an excuse to back out.

"Oh, no. Don't make me your scapegoat," Travis drawled. "If you and my brother want to sing together, go ahead and do it."

Listening to the sound of his footsteps on the stairs a moment later, Rory asked herself what she had really expected him to do—fall into a jealous rage, forbid her to spend time with any male other than himself and then declare his undying love?

She had to grin at her own wishful thinking as she admitted to herself that, deep down, it was precisely the reaction she'd hoped for.

After dinner, Travis excused himself and headed upstairs. The whole time Rory was cleaning up the kitchen, she could hear the squeak of floorboards from overhead as though he was pacing. When she finally dried her hands and turned out the light, intending to see what he was up to, he headed her off in the hall and suggested they watch a movie together on the VCR. Stifling her curiosity, she agreed.

Nearly two hours later, Travis switched off the television and looked at her from where he sat in the oversize leather recliner. "Ready for bed?" His tone was light, but his expression was similar to that of a bull calf she'd seen at the fall roundup—a mixture of dread and resignation.

Stifling a yawn, Rory complied.

"You go on," he said as he got to his feet. "I'll just lock up down here."

They hardly ever locked the doors. Disappointed at the transparency of his stalling technique, she went slowly up the stairs. When she got to her room, the first thing she noticed was that the bed had been stripped. Pressing a trembling hand to her stomach, she stared at the bare nightstand and the empty closet.

Was he kicking her out? Was this his reply to her announcement that she and Charlie were performing a duet for the congregation? Could he be that cruel?

She heard his footsteps approaching and the squeak of the hinges on the door to his room. For a moment,

Rory kept staring at her denuded bedroom. Then, slowly, fury beat out the hurt she was getting heartily sick of dealing with. If he thought he was going to hide in his own room and avoid a confrontation over this, he'd better think again.

Coming to a sudden decision, she stormed down the hall, slapped open the door to his room and burst inside, ready to tell him exactly what she thought of his tactics.

The sight that greeted Rory stalled her in her tracks. Her mouth hung open and her eyes filled with tears.

Travis was perched on the edge of his mattress, his expression downright forbidding. On the bed rested her missing pillow, right next to his. Spread out on the quilt was one of her nighties. On one of the bed tables sat her clock, the paperback she'd been reading and a small framed photo of her parents.

"Oh, Travis." It was all she could say.

He was watching her with a somber expression. "Do you mind?" he asked, getting to his feet. "I thought perhaps it was time, but maybe I was wrong to rush things."

"No," she said with a watery smile, "you weren't wrong."

Slowly, Travis's fierce expression softened and he held out his arms.

Bless Charlie and his crazy ideas, she thought distractedly, and then she catapulted herself into her husband's embrace.

When his clock radio went off the next morning, Travis rolled over and slapped it quiet without opening his eyes. The hour had been late when they'd finally gone to sleep, and later still when he'd wakened his wife again. Her passion had run as hot as his own, leaving him both sated and starving for more. Now he pried open one eye and turned his head to meet Rory's sleepy gaze.

"Morning," he whispered. "Sleep well?"

With a murmur of satisfaction, she slid closer and spread one warm hand on his bare chest. "I think so," she muttered as his senses sprang alive at her touch. "Is this morning?"

"'Fraid so." He dreaded the idea of leaving their love nest and facing the cold. The weatherman had predicted a sharp drop in the temperature the night before and snow by the end of the week. Preparing for winter was hard, heavy work, but surely he had earned himself a morning off. And Rory hadn't run screaming from his bed, not yet.

He reached for the phone on his nightstand.

"What are you doing?" she asked, pressing her face into her pillow.

"Calling Adam. How about breakfast in town? Afterward, we could stop by the video store and pick up a couple of movies if you'd like."

Her head popped up. "Really? You'd take some time off?" Her eyes were sparkling, making him realize just how little he'd done to please her since their hasty wedding. How little it took to make her happy.

"No one's indispensable," he drawled as Adam's voice came on the line. As soon as Travis had made his excuses, surprised Adam didn't argue, he turned back over in the big, warm bed. Rory was watching him with a lazy smile on her mouth and a gleam in her eyes.

"So," he said, reassessing the situation, "how do you feel about lunch in town instead of breakfast?"

She wasn't about to question the sudden, drastic change in Travis's attitude; she was too sated by his lovemaking, too busy enjoying his attention to care overmuch what had caused it. Ever since the night he'd moved her things into his room, he'd made a point to be home on time for dinner and to spend part of each evening with her. They watched television or a video, read compatibly as they listened to music. They'd even picked some new CDs from a catalog, a mixture of the country sounds she was learning to enjoy and the easy, mellow rock she wanted to share with him.

When they climbed the stairs together, hands linked, Rory's world narrowed to him, just him. After they made love, he'd gather her close, arms tight around her. Some women might need words, but Rory felt him slide into sleep like a child and she savored the intimacy of a man who didn't trust easily, trusting her.

At Charlie's insistence, she'd gone with him one evening to audition for the choir director. Despite her nervousness, Mr. Stanley had granted his enthusiastic approval.

Adam had a piano at his house. Kim took lessons, and Charlie dabbled with easy competence. Rory went there several times to practice with him before regular rehearsals began. He must have been mistaken about Travis's jealousy; he showed little interest in the project at all.

Tonight when he'd come home, smelling of leather,

sweat and outdoor air, he'd swept her into his arms and pressed his cold cheek to hers, eyes glittering possessively before he kissed her. When he bounded up the stairs, she thought happily she could do this every day without getting bored. Feeding her man, spending time with him, sleeping in his arms—dreaming of a future spent together. Life at its most basic level.

She glanced out the window at the gathering darkness. There was more of his life she intended to share besides meals and sex and church, but that would all come in time.

Suddenly her stomach curled over on itself, threatening to heave out its contents. Head spinning, she rushed for the downstairs bathroom and barely made it before she was violently ill.

As quickly as the nausea had come, it subsided. Rory rinsed her mouth, looking in the mirror at the reflection of her sheet-white skin and dark, haunted eyes.

She hoped she hadn't caught some bug. Being sick was a nuisance.

Hearing Travis's footsteps on the stairs, she pinched color into her cheeks and hurried back to the kitchen. When they sat down to eat the beef stew she'd fixed with buttermilk biscuits and a molded salad, her head and her appetite were steady. Skipping lunch must have soured her stomach.

Relieved, she passed bowls and watched Travis. If his relaxed expression was any indication, marriage seemed to agree with him.

"How was your day?" she asked, spoon poised.

He took a swallow of milk. "Cold. Weather's

changing. If we get an early snowfall, we'll have to start hauling feed for the cattle. They don't forage like horses. They'll stand around and starve.''

''I could help,'' Rory offered. ''Tending the house doesn't take all my time, and Flynn's made it clear he doesn't want me messing in his kitchen.'' Not since word of her marriage to the boss had spread. Now the men were all a little uncomfortable around her, but she was confident that would pass in time.

''You don't need to cook for the men anymore,'' Travis said possessively.

''But I could still help you,'' she persisted. ''Ranch wives do their share.'' She knew from the way the women at church talked that they turned a hand to whatever needed doing. Putting in a garden in the spring, raising kids, rounding up strays, making jam, birthing calves, doctoring sick animals—she was looking forward to it all.

An image formed in her mind of her and Travis with their children, two boys and two girls. He'd want children, she mused. There was a lot of love in him waiting to be tapped, like a sugar maple tree.

''Hauling hay and cake in the snow is hard, miserable work,'' Travis warned her as the image dissolved. ''The wind slices through however many layers you think will keep you warm. The snow melts and you get soaked. The bales are heavy, and the cows would walk right over you to get at the feed.''

''I don't care.''

He studied her thoughtfully for a moment, and then he broke open a steaming biscuit. ''When the time comes, we'll see if you still want to,'' he said as he spread butter.

She'd have to be content with that. "Okay." She noticed he was still fiddling with the biscuit. "Something on your mind?" she asked.

His smile still set her pulse to thrumming, that and the lazy hunger she could read in his eyes. "Getting to read me pretty well," he said. "I don't know that I care for that."

"You're getting to know me, too," she reminded him with a flutter of lashes. "There's one thing you always seem to know I'm thinking about."

His eyes darkened, and his attention settled on her mouth for a moment. "Because I think about it, too." His voice was low and husky. Then, as longing swept through her, he blinked and his lips twitched. "Hell's bells, woman, you know how to distract a man."

"Sorry," she murmured saucily. "I guess I'll just have to behave myself."

"Don't reform on my account," he replied. Then he began busily dissecting a piece of carrot with his fork as carefully as if it were a biology class specimen. "Tell me about Daniel."

The sudden request caught Rory off guard. Staring hard at her plate, she collected her thoughts. Travis hadn't mentioned the phone message again; she'd assumed he'd forgotten all about it.

"Do you mind talking about him?" he asked around a bite of biscuit.

"Of course I don't mind," Rory said a little too quickly. "I should have told you about him before." Daniel seemed a part of her very distant past. She hadn't called him back, and he hadn't bothered her again. Knowing him, he'd probably been between waitresses when he'd left the message for Rory.

She blotted her mouth with her napkin and set it back in her lap, twisting her fingers in its folds. Briefly, she explained how she'd married Daniel and gone to work in the family diner, staying on after their divorce. "His parents seemed like family," she explained, "and I was comfortable with the job."

"You and your ex-husband got along pretty well?" Travis probed.

Rory shrugged. "For the most part." And almost too well at the end, but she couldn't tell Travis that.

He merely raised an eyebrow and resumed eating.

"I answered Charlie's ad on a whim," she recalled. The summer had been humid and hot and predictable, right from the start. She'd been restless and bored, flirting with a serious case of discontent and looking for some innocent fun. "His letters described a world I knew nothing about. It was all so fascinating to me."

"How long did you write?"

"For several months. Then he invited me to visit him," Rory recalled. "New York can be a real hell-hole in the summer, but Colorado seemed like another world. At first I turned him down."

"What changed your mind?" Travis asked.

She swallowed the sudden lump in her throat. Admitting her own gullibility was difficult. "The Mancinis sold the diner. The rest of us weren't informed until the new owners were ready to take over. Suddenly, we were all out of work." When she'd seen the severance check in her pay envelope, Rory realized she'd been kidding herself. She hadn't really been part of the Mancini family since her divorce from Daniel five years before.

"Just like that, they let you go?" Travis asked.

"They gave me a severance check. It should have been enough to tide me over until I found something else."

Travis laid down his fork. "Should have been? What happened?"

This was the hard part. "One of my customers knew someone with an investment deal," she said slowly, forcing out the words. "He'd already made a bundle, and he was eager to share the opportunity with me. Daniel gave him my number, and he introduced me to the investor."

Travis groaned and shook his head.

"I know what you're thinking," she said. "But I made a good return on the severance money, so I reinvested that along with the rest of my savings."

Travis reached out and covered her hand with his. "What happened?"

"The two of them were in cahoots. They pulled the same scam on a lot of people and then they left town with the money." She shrugged. "I wasn't the only fool they took advantage of." Her laugh was shaky. "Some consolation, huh? They're living it up in some country without extradition laws." She could remember how overwhelmed she'd felt at the time—her job was gone, her savings were gone, and she'd nearly slept with her ex-husband.

"Charlie's invitation must have looked pretty good after all you went through." Travis let go of her hand.

"It wasn't like that," Rory exclaimed. "Charlie knew about the money. Too bad I didn't tell him about the investment deal until it was too late. Maybe he would have talked me out of it. After it went sour, he sent me a ticket to Denver.'' It had been her idea to burn her bridges, not his. If she told Travis that, he'd think she'd married him out of desperation.

She had, but he'd never believe she'd been falling desperately in love with him. Not after what she'd just told him.

''If Charlie hadn't taken off the way he did, you might have married him,'' Travis said.

She tossed her napkin on the table and slid back her chair. ''If things had been different, I don't know what I might have done.'' Honesty forced her admission. ''But I didn't marry Charlie, I married you.''

Travis took his dishes to the counter. She would have given a lot to know what he was thinking. ''Maybe that's only added to your problems,'' he said gruffly.

Rory's eyes misted at his wistful tone. Without thinking, she flew into his arms and pressed her cheek to his shoulder. ''Don't say that. Don't think it. Marrying you has made me happy.''

For a moment, he held her tight. ''I hope you always feel that way,'' he said roughly as he let her go. ''I have some paperwork I can't put off, but I'll try not to be too long.''

Travis spent the rest of the evening in his office, but he didn't get much work done. Instead, he wasted a lot of time staring at numbers that made no sense while he thought about everything Rory had told him.

Desperation had brought him a bride. Would that be enough to keep them together? He didn't think of himself as an introspective man, but he was savvy enough to know she'd wormed her way into his life.

Losing her would leave a hole he might never be able to fill, and that scared the hell out of him.

He was trying to make the most of his unconventional marriage, but he wasn't sure he knew how. She said she was happy. Did he dare to hope he could keep her that way? If he lost her, would he lose what was left of his heart, as well?

Frustrated, he closed the folder he'd been pretending to study and went back downstairs. When he found Rory curled in a corner of the couch with a book, legs tucked under her, he felt a wave of relief. She looked up, a concerned expression on her face that fled as soon as he produced a smile.

"Come to bed," he said gruffly, holding out his hand. He had a sudden desperate need to hold her close, to make her his, at least for now.

Instantly, she closed the book, unfolded her long legs and scrambled to her feet. Her cheeks colored prettily as she took his hand. Travis had no choice; he swept her into his arms and kissed her, pouring into the embrace all the feelings he couldn't find the courage to put into words.

Chapter Eleven

"Sorry, boys, three ladies wins." Charlie tossed down his cards and raked in the small pile of chips in the center of the table, nearly upsetting the bottle at his elbow.

Barney slid his chair back. "That's it for me," he said with a good-natured grin. "I'm outta here before I end up giving back all my pay." Swaying, he picked up his shot glass and tossed back its contents. "Mighty fine bourbon, boss." He saluted Adam with the empty glass.

Adam muttered a reply as Flynn put out his cigar and got unsteadily to his feet. "Can you drop me off?" he asked Barney, stuffing his change into his pocket. "I'm tapped out."

Travis watched the others through a pleasant haze as he took a long pull from his beer bottle. They were gathered at Adam's for their quarterly poker party, boys' night in, and his head was growing fuzzy from the beer and smoke. He glanced down at the skimpy pile of chips in front of him. It had definitely been Charlie's night.

Adam finished his cola and stood up. ''We might as well call it a night. Why don't I drive both of you?'' he suggested. ''Barney, you can get your truck in the morning.''

Barney must have realized he was in no shape to argue. Normally none of the men were heavy drinkers. ''Sure,'' he replied with a shrug. ''Jane can bring me back over.''

Adam settled his hat on his head and reached for his jacket. ''You two can let yourselves out,'' he told Charlie and Travis. ''I'll see you tomorrow.''

After the others had left, Charlie eyed the small pile of chips in front of Travis and his own winnings. ''How about one more hand?'' he asked. ''Double or nothing.''

Travis looked up at the clock and tried to make out the numbers. Part of him wanted to crawl into bed with his wife; part wanted to come away from the game with a chunk of his brother's money.

Charlie shuffled the cards. ''You in?'' he asked.

''Why not?''

Somehow, during the deal, Rory's name came up. Travis wasn't sure how. One minute he was looking at his cards, pleased to see a possible straight looking back. The next, he and Charlie were on their feet, nose to nose.

''Find a woman of your own,'' he heard himself say.

Charlie's grin wavered in front of him, all teeth. "Seems like she was mine first," he taunted.

How many beers had Travis consumed? He should have known better; he had no head for booze. Suddenly he realized he really wanted to punch someone. Charlie's smile made a tempting target. "And now she's mine."

"Don't get your Skivvies in a knot," Charlie scolded. "I may be the better man, but all she and I are is friends." He crossed his chest in a sloppy X. "I swear."

Travis snorted in disbelief and his fingers twitched. "You brought her out here," he accused, as if that in itself was a sin.

Charlie's grin seemed to grow wider. "Can't help it if she still prefers my company to yours. Women do, you know."

He pushed the one button Travis himself had been tapping on for too long. Fury descended like a red curtain. Before he knew his own intentions, his fist had shot out and whistled past Charlie's right ear.

Abruptly, Charlie's grin faded. "That was too close." He reared back and threw a punch of his own.

Travis dodged, but not in time. Charlie's fist clipped his chin and his teeth snapped together. He staggered, stomach executing a lazy roll as the room spun. Righting himself, he gave his head a hard shake to clear it. In a blink, the beer haze was gone. His own aim was truer now, his knuckles hitting flesh and bone with a satisfying smack.

Charlie stepped back, his hand to his eye, and tripped over a chair. Travis moved in, bloodlust pumping, and watched for another opening as Charlie got to his feet.

"Come on," Travis coaxed, motioning Charlie closer. Travis was the one who'd taught him to defend himself, so they knew each other's moves as well as their own.

They traded a couple more blows, and then finally, winded, they separated. Travis's ribs ached and it hurt to breathe. There was a tear in his sleeve. He was too old for fighting, and it never settled a confounded thing.

"Damn," Charlie exclaimed, blinking hard, "I think you nailed me good, brother."

Travis's knuckles were starting to throb. He'd forgotten just how painful a good go-round could be. Keeping his gaze on Charlie, he wiggled his jaw back and forth. It ached, but Charlie's eye was already swelling shut.

"Better get some ice on that," Travis suggested. He'd rather be staked to an anthill than admit it was he who needed the ice for his hand.

Straightening, Charlie surprised Travis by giving his back a friendly slap as he headed for the ice bucket. "Feel better now?" he asked after he'd dug out a couple of cubes and wrapped them in a napkin. Gingerly, he held it to his eye. "You been spoiling for this."

"You been asking," Travis snapped, ignoring the hand his brother stuck out and plunging his into the ice bucket instead. His gut was churning with the violence he still felt. Now that common sense was beginning to return, he wondered how Mrs. Clark and Kim had slept through the commotion. Good thing both their rooms were at the opposite end of the large house.

"There's something you need to know," Charlie said quietly. "Maybe I should have told you sooner, but I just didn't think you'd actually marry her before I got back."

The change in his voice drew Travis's attention. His head was starting to pound and his fingers ached. Dropping into a chair, he set the ice bucket on the table in front of him. When he looked at his brother's misshapen face, shame and frustration rose in his craw like shards of glass. Fighting never solved anything, but for a few hot moments he'd wanted desperately to draw blood. Winchester blood.

"What is it?" Travis growled defensively.

Charlie pulled out another chair and set down his makeshift ice pack. He started fiddling with his empty beer bottle.

A chill ran through Travis. "Are you okay?" he demanded. "Is something wrong with you?" Had Charlie really left for some medical reason he hadn't revealed? Travis gritted his teeth, sending a shooting pain through his injured jaw.

"I brought her here for you," Charlie burst out, just as Adam walked through the door. Looking from one man to the other, he froze in his tracks.

"Who won?" he asked dryly.

Charlie glanced at Travis. "I think it was a draw."

Ignoring Adam, Travis slapped the table with his good hand to corral Charlie's attention. "What did you say?" he demanded, leaning forward. "You brought who where?"

For once, Charlie's grin wasn't in evidence. "Well,

you weren't meeting any women,'' he said with a shrug. ''I figured you had to be lonely.'' He looked at Adam. ''Didn't you think he was lonely? You saw how he was, never going to town, never making an effort to meet anyone. Never going out.''

''Oh, no,'' Adam drawled, retreating. ''You aren't dragging me into this.''

Travis had started to rise, not sure if he wanted to hit Charlie again or merely choke him. ''My life was going just fine,'' he snarled. ''Perhaps you'd better explain why you thought it was any of your concern.''

Charlie swallowed, the muscles in his throat jumping, and licked his lips. ''That's a crock and we both know it. You'll thank me, eventually. I decided last spring after you ditched Nancy Larson that something needed to be done, so I ran an ad for a wife in some singles' magazine.''

''I didn't dump Nancy,'' Travis muttered, half to himself. What had happened between them? Funny, he didn't even remember. They'd drifted apart. Last he'd heard, she'd gotten engaged to a dentist from Sterling.

Charlie went on as if Travis hadn't interrupted. ''Writing to Rory was fun. She's smart, great looking. Well, you know that.'' Again he glanced at Adam.

''I think we can all agree she's a doll,'' Adam drawled.

''Not really my type,'' Charlie continued, speaking to Travis once again, ''but I thought you might hit it off if I could arrange a meeting.'' He started peeling the label from the bottle he'd been passing from one hand to the other while Travis waited for him to get to whatever point he was trying to make. ''I never thought she'd actually come out here, but some things changed for her and suddenly she was on her way. I knew my presence would only cloud things, so I cleared out.'' Charlie's grin came back, but his gaze darted nervously between his brothers. ''I guess Nature did the rest.''

From the doorway, Adam swore softly. ''Don't kill him,'' he instructed Travis. ''And don't make a lot of noise. I'm going up to bed.''

After he left, Travis stood looking at Charlie with a dozen different thoughts running through his head. The fight was gone out of him, but he wasn't sure what had taken its place. He was still trying to deal with the idea of his baby brother finding him a woman. When he had more energy, he'd be furious.

For now, the situation might be funny if he hadn't fallen for her.

''Does Rory know about this?'' he asked.

''She wasn't in on it, if that's what you're wondering. Before she came, we just said we'd see what happened.''

Which was pretty much what she'd told him, but it didn't tell Travis a damn thing about her feelings for Charlie. Had she married her second choice? The idea nearly killed him.

''So, uh, how does she feel about me?'' he demanded, shoving aside his pride. Who knew better than Charlie?

He must have sensed that Travis wasn't going to pound him. ''Don't you know?''

Travis wasn't used to talking about feelings. The subject made him uncomfortable. ''We got married in a hurry,'' he admitted reluctantly. ''We skipped over a lot.''

Charlie chuckled and shook his head. ''If you want to know how your wife feels about you, why don't you ask her?''

The idea was too damned scary. What if he didn't like her answer? ''I can't do that.''

''Then tell her how *you* feel,'' Charlie suggested. ''Women really go for stuff like that.''

Travis was sick of Charlie telling him what women liked. ''You don't have any idea how I feel.''

Charlie's grin was so wide his dimples flashed like extra belly buttons. ''A blind man could see that you're head over heels.'' He puffed out his chest. ''Can I pick a woman for you or not?''

''Don't break your arm patting yourself on the back,'' Travis grumbled darkly. ''It will take a miracle to make this marriage work.''

Charlie got up and circled the table. He rested a brotherly hand on Travis's shoulder. ''Then make a miracle, bro, because when it comes to picking out women, Charlie's never wrong.''

Rory sank to her knees, clutching the porcelain bowl as she waited for the spinning sensation to subside. Around her the house was quiet, but Travis would be home any moment. She had to pull herself together before he got here and saw her like this.

First thing this morning, as soon as he was gone, she'd used the pregnancy test she'd smuggled home from the drugstore. Until she'd seen the results for herself, she'd assumed her system was merely adjusting to all the recent changes in her life.

Groaning, she pulled herself to her feet. It must have happened that first time. They'd been careful since then.

How was she going to tell Travis? How would he react to the news? They still had so many other issues to resolve. Would he feel trapped or elated by this new development?

Traditional male that he was, he'd done the right thing and married her. Now he'd bite the bullet again and she'd never know for sure how he really felt.

A tear rolled down her cheek as she wiped her flushed face with a cool, wet cloth. She wanted a husband who loved her, not one who felt trapped by honor and circumstances.

The sound from the kitchen alerted her to Travis's arrival. With a final glance in the mirror, she went to greet him.

It was Charlie, not Travis, who stood in the kitchen.

"What happened to your eye?" Rory asked. It was purple and swollen half-shut.

He made a dismissive gesture. "Little disagreement," he said. "Nothing serious."

Had he gotten into an argument with one of the men? Someone in town? It was easy to see he wasn't about to become any more forthcoming.

"I knocked," he said, idly scratching his jaw, "but you didn't answer. Are you okay?"

She'd nearly forgotten her own problem, at least for a moment. Was there a readable change on her face? In her eyes? "I'm fine," she replied nervously. "Why do you ask?"

"Because you were too busy being sick to hear me come in." He was frowning, a line pleating his forehead and adding to the distortion of his features. "Why don't you tell me what's going on?"

"Going on?" she echoed. What if he voiced his concerns to Travis?

"Yeah, honey," he said. "It's all over your face. Do you want me to draw my own conclusions? It wouldn't be difficult."

His comment made her hands fly to her cheeks as if she could hide whatever he saw there. Did she have *pregnant* stamped on her forehead?

Rory braced her hands behind her on the kitchen counter. She needed to confide in someone. Telling her former mother-in-law didn't seem appropriate. Charlie was her closest friend in Colorado. Could she trust him to keep his mouth shut?

Nibbling her lip indecisively, Rory stared at the salt and pepper set she'd bought with the idea of charming Travis into loving her. How naive she'd been to think fixing up the house would make a difference to him. Tears blurred her eyes.

She'd never cried so easily until she came to Colorado. Was this one of the symptoms she'd have to endure for the next eight months or so?

"Something upset my stomach," she hedged, without looking up.

"Something like a baby?" Charlie asked gently.

"Aren't you jumping to conclusions?" she countered.

"Am I? You're pale, you're tired, and you look wrung out half the time."

"Thank you very much. You've just disproved your theory. Haven't you heard that pregnant women glow?" she exclaimed, annoyed at his harsh assessment.

"Is that why you and Travis got married so quickly?"

She looked up, aghast. "No! He has no idea—" Abruptly, she pressed her lips together, but it was too late.

"Aha!" Charlie exclaimed.

"Promise me you won't say anything," Rory pleaded. "Swear it. Travis should hear it from me."

Charlie hesitated. "Of course he should. You have to tell him, and soon. He has a right to know."

The tears started falling in earnest. "How?" she cried. "He'll feel more trapped than he does already. How can I tell him?"

Charlie crossed the kitchen and pulled her into his arms.

It was that way Travis found them. They sprang apart when he walked in the back door, guilt stamped on their faces as plain as the Winchester brand. He barely noticed that Rory looked as though she'd been crying.

Dumbfounded, he stopped in his tracks. "What the hell is going on here?"

"It's not what you think," she burst out, face red and blotchy.

Charlie moved so he was standing partly in front of her. The idea that he might think she needed protection from her own husband sucked the heat from Travis's anger until he felt as though he'd been turned to ice. He'd never raised his fists against a woman and he never would. His brother might prove to be a different story, but for now Travis was still in shock.

"Don't worry," he drawled, acid burning holes in his gut as he brushed past them. "Neither of you is worth my time. As far as I'm concerned, you deserve each other."

"Travis!" Rory's voice was filled with shock. What did she expect from him now?

And Charlie. Travis had been feeling guilty about blackening his brother's eye, but now he was coldly pleased it looked so bad. Everything he'd told Travis the night before had been a bald-faced lie.

He stopped in the doorway. They were still frozen in place like wax mannequins. Rory was pale, and Charlie's cheeks had flushed a dull red that clashed badly with his bruised eye.

"If you want each other," Travis said slowly, the numbness already draining away as pain began to radiate outward from the heart he was sure had shattered into a million pieces, each one piercing the wall of his chest, "it means nothing to me, understand?" He made a sweeping gesture with his hand. "Maybe you'd better move back in, bro, and *I'll* move out."

Right before he spun away, he saw Rory sway, saw

Charlie's hands reach out to steady her. Afraid that he might go after his brother after all, Travis lunged up the stairs.

He heard her call his name again, but he ignored her.

"Give him some time to cool off," Charlie was saying. "I'll try talking to him later."

Nauseated by the reassurance in his tone, Travis wanted to shout for him to forget trying. Charlie, the great manipulator, the ladies' man and expert on women. Compared to the hurt and betrayal Travis felt now, what he'd gone through in school was only a faint, unpleasant memory.

After Travis went stomping out of the kitchen, Charlie insisted Rory go with him to Adam's house. "I'm not leaving you here alone with Travis," he insisted. "Not in your condition. I don't think you'd be in any real danger, not for a minute, but he needs some time alone. Later we'll face him together and make him see the truth."

Rory was too upset to argue. Behind the anger on Travis's face, she had thought she'd glimpsed a flash of real pain. For a moment, her heart had soared with hope that he did care. Then the fire in his eyes had blanked out, taking with it her spurt of elation. If he'd had any feelings for her at all, she had just killed them as surely as if she really *had* been doing something wrong.

Automatically, she glanced at the stove. Earlier she'd cooked a ham, with baked beans and scalloped potatoes. ''What about supper?'' she asked distractedly. ''Travis needs to eat.''

"I don't think he's very hungry,'' Charlie said gently. ''Why don't you just turn off the oven for now.''

Like a robot, she complied. From overhead, the floor squeaked beneath her husband's footsteps. If her relationship with him had been more secure, built on a solid foundation of trust and weathered by time, this misunderstanding would never have happened. Instead, she might have been lying in his arms right now and telling him about the baby.

Time, she thought, laying a protective hand on her stomach. It seemed as though, for them, time was one commodity that had just run out.

''Come on,'' Charlie urged, tugging at her arm. ''You're as pale as a bucket of snow. You need to rest.''

As Rory followed Charlie to his shiny red truck, her thoughts circled bitterly. She'd been worried Travis might feel trapped; now she was terrified that he would hate her and their unborn child.

''How could you be so stupid?'' Adam demanded, his contemptuous gaze riveted on Charlie. The three of them were seated in Adam's living room and he had banished Kim upstairs.

''It wasn't Charlie's fault,'' Rory interjected.

Adam raked a hand over his black hair. ''Charlie knows Travis has always felt a little insecure around him.'' He sounded exasperated. ''It's no secret that

Travis wasn't popular with girls in school, while Charlie had to beat them off with a stick.''

At his words, Charlie turned crimson and looked away. ''I had no idea how he felt at the time,'' he muttered.

''You should have bent over backward to avoid this kind of situation,'' Adam retorted. ''As for this hare-brained scheme of yours to bring them together in the first place—'' He broke off and bowed his head, muttering a string of curses.

''Rory wasn't in on that,'' Charlie exclaimed. ''She would never have gone along with it.''

''So you just didn't tell her,'' Adam sneered. ''Don't you ever decide to do anything like that to me.'' He waved a threatening finger. ''I'd string you up, and not by the neck.'' He looked apologetically at Rory. ''Not that you aren't a perfectly nice woman,'' he began, ''but Charlie was way out of line.''

''I love him,'' Rory blurted.

Adam's eyes widened. ''Charlie?''

''No, Travis.'' She twisted her hands together in her lap, feeling as fragile as a spun sugar cake decoration. ''I'm in love with him. That's why I married him when he asked.'' She certainly had a talent for picking the wrong men. First Daniel with the roving eye and now Travis, whose ability to trust had apparently left along with his mother when he'd been just a child.

Adam sat back and studied her for a moment. ''Actually, I assumed that. Now, what are you going to do about it?''

It was her turn to stare. ''Do?'' she echoed.

He got to his feet and began pacing restlessly. The room was certainly large enough for pacing, or just about anything else a person or a group of people might want to do in it. Overhead, the ceiling soared. One wall was glass, another was covered by a fireplace made of river rock. The carpet beneath their feet was an impractical vanilla, thick as heavy cream, and the furniture was done in pastels. Rory had barely noticed when she first came in; now she looked around distractedly as she tried to figure out how to answer Adam's question.

''He caught you in a compromising position with his brother,'' Adam continued ruthlessly. ''Now he's more or less condemned you without a trial. Maybe if you go back on your hands and knees, grovel enough, he'll allow you to explain what really happened. If you're convincing, he might even listen, but your humility and remorse need work. You sure can't go back with a chip on your pretty shoulder and demand that he trust you just because he's your husband.'' Adam's expression was somber, rational. He shrugged. ''After all, why should he?''

Rory leaped to her feet, provoked beyond her endurance. If she hadn't been pregnant, if she had just been sick and feeling lousy, she never would have stood for Travis's temper tantrum, not for a second. And as for his accusations, she should have stuffed them right back down his throat.

"Where are you going?" Charlie asked, standing.

"To talk to my husband," Rory replied through clenched teeth. "He and I have a few things to discuss."

Adam grinned, putting a detaining hand on Charlie's arm when he would have followed her. "Don't forget about the groveling and apologizing," he goaded. "Guys love that."

Rory hissed in a breath and shot Adam a look that would have parched corn. "Sure I will," she snarled. "Right after I break off his arm and beat him with it."

"Wait a minute," Charlie said. "I don't think—"

"That's right," she snapped. "*Don't* think. Men! You can't live without them and you can't kill them."

"Hey, Rory," Adam said as she was about to slam out the fancy front door.

"What?" Impatiently she turned just in time to catch the keys he tossed her.

"Take my truck."

When she pulled up behind Travis's house, hitting the brakes so hard the bed of the truck fishtailed, she was ready to have it out with him. The only trouble was, his pickup was nowhere in sight. She stormed inside on the chance that he might be home, anyway, but the silence in the house was absolute.

He hadn't touched the food she left for him. Panic blocking her throat like rising bread dough, she raced upstairs. The door to his room stood open. Going through to the bathroom, she saw that his toothbrush and razor were missing. A more thorough search of the bedroom told her he'd taken some clothes with him, too.

What was it about her that Winchester men kept leaving? she wondered on a near hysterical bubble of laughter. First Charlie and now Travis. Was Adam next?

Wild with frustration, she spun around in a circle, searching for something on which to vent her emotion. Confound it, where had he gone? How dare he not be here for her to tell him exactly what she thought of his distrust, his indifference. His refusal to love her.

Rory stumbled to a stop, her energy draining away and leaving her as limp and empty as a rag doll whose stuffing had leaked out. Sinking down on the edge of the bed, she bit her lip and fought off the tears of frustration that threatened. If she had her way, she'd never cry over Travis Winchester again.

Chapter Twelve

"You won't talk to Charlie, you won't talk to me," Adam said as he heaved a bale of hay off the back of the pickup. "You have to talk to someone."

Silently, Travis cut the wire on the bale and began spreading it for the hungry cattle. It was two weeks before Thanksgiving and a recent storm had dumped well over a foot of snow on the ground. The highway had been shut down off and on, and some flights at the airport were canceled. At the ranch, teams of men had been out all morning spreading hay and cake for the cattle. Temperatures were expected to drop.

Adam tossed another bale off the tailgate, narrowly missing Travis.

"Hey!" he exclaimed as the hay landed at his feet. "Watch what you're doing."

"He speaks." Adam's voice was laced with sarcasm.

Travis glared. Adam stared back at him, clearly unperturbed by Travis's bad temper. The wind picked up, blowing bits of snow that stung Travis's cheeks like biting flies. Finally he turned away as a determined steer butted him hard with its head. "Dinner's coming," he snarled at the animal as he bent over the bale. "Don't knock me down."

Despite his heavy gloves, his hands were so cold they ached. His feet were growing numb in their insulated boots, and the wind had found the thin strip of bare skin between his collar and his stocking cap.

"That's the last of it," Adam said, jumping down from the truck and brushing his gloves together.

Travis didn't reply, but he was mighty glad they were done. Compared to the frigid outside air, the cab of the truck would be cozy, its heater pouring out warmth to thaw his frigid limbs all the way back to the barn. He didn't want to think about the rest of his day, dinner in the bunkhouse kitchen followed by a restless hour or two playing checkers with Gus or mending tack—anything to kill time until it was finally late enough to turn in so he could spend a sleepless night on a narrow bed. With Charlie staying with Adam, and Rory back at his own house, he had nowhere else to go.

Just as Travis straightened from breaking up the last bale of hay, a snowball whizzed past his head.

"What the hell?" He turned, catching the next one full in the face. Blinded, he wiped away the wet, cold snow as Adam's laughter triggered the pent-up frustration and resentment Travis had been nursing since he'd caught Rory and Charlie together.

With a roar of pure rage, he lowered his head and

charged. Adam's laughter turned to a grunt of surprise as Travis's momentum tumbled them both in the snow.

Arms wrapped around each other in a grotesque parody of an embrace, the two men rolled over and over on the lumpy ground. Exchanging blows was futile; they were sandwiched too close together. Finally Travis broke away and staggered to his feet, spitting out snow as he cocked his fists.

Adam got up, hampered as Travis was by his heavy clothing. "Had enough?" he asked coolly.

Travis's answer was to dive at him again. Beneath his feet, the rut in the road was full of ice. His feet slipped and his punch went wild. He landed hard on one knee. The jolt snapped his teeth together and bloodied his tongue. Winded, he shook his head to clear it. What the hell was he thinking? All he did lately was fight.

He looked up to see Adam's outstretched hand. Embarrassed, Travis clasped it and hauled himself up. His knee protested, and he tasted blood from his mangled tongue. Hell's bells, he still had a couple of bruises from his scuffle with Charlie.

"Come on," Adam said, clapping his back. "There's still coffee left in the thermos. I think we could use some."

While Adam started the truck, Travis held a handful of snow to his sore knee. When it started to soak through his jeans he discarded it and climbed in the cab.

"Thanks," he muttered as Adam handed him a steaming mug. No apologies were forthcoming, but Travis couldn't meet his brother's gaze. Instead, he stared out the passenger window, sipping his coffee as the silence grew.

Adam rolled down his window and tossed out the dregs from his mug. "Do you really think Charlie would touch your wife?" he asked bluntly.

Travis gritted his teeth. He'd been ignoring the obvious answer to that question for a week. "Of course not," he growled, facing the truth he'd known since the first jealous rage had subsided.

"Then it must be Rory you distrust," Adam reasoned in as pleasant a tone as if he'd been discussing the weather. More pleasant; the weather was lousy.

Travis turned in the seat so quickly he nearly dumped coffee in his lap. He opened his mouth to defend her, and then saw the trap Adam had laid.

"When Christie left, I let you brood in peace," Travis said bitterly. "Why can't you give me the same courtesy?"

Adam sat back against the door, big hands wrapped around his empty mug. His gaze was steady, making Travis want to squirm. "Maybe it's *because* I brooded alone that I'm trying to get you to talk," he said. "What is it that you're afraid of?"

"Who says I'm afraid?" Travis countered with automatic bravado.

Adam's grin was all-knowing. "I've been there, man. All the way there and back. You can't bluff me. You're scared to death."

For a long moment, Travis hung on to his pride, and then he folded like a gambler with a bad poker hand.

"I'm afraid Rory will leave me." His voice

sounded harsh to his own ears, as if it had been rubbed raw.

"Why do you think that?" Adam probed. "Has she threatened to go? I thought she was settling in pretty nicely."

"She's a city woman, born and bred," Travis countered. "Mama left, Christie left. She'll go, too." He looked out the windshield at the unbroken expanse of white, sky and land so pale the horizon line was blurred. He loved this country. He'd been born on it; he'd die on it. Spending winters here was how you earned the springs.

"I don't want Rory to leave," he muttered, half to himself.

"Rory's not Mama, and the good Lord knows she's not Christie," Adam replied. "If you haven't yet told her that you *want* her to stay, maybe it's time you two had a serious talk." When Travis didn't reply, he set his mug on the dash and put the truck in gear. "I'm here, you know," he added. "If you need anything."

"Yeah, thanks." Travis drained the rest of his cold coffee. Trust Adam to make everything sound so easy, he thought with silent irritation as they bounced and slid down the road. *Just talk to her.* Only problem was, Travis had no idea what to say.

"Is she okay?" he thought to ask. "Rory? Have you seen her?" He'd driven by the house several times, but he hadn't gone in. He knew Adam or Charlie would have checked on her. So far the power hadn't gone out, or the phones.

"She's been rehearsing for the pageant a lot,"

Adam replied, correcting a skid before the truck could slide off the road. "Are you going?"

Travis shrugged. Of course he'd go, even if it tore a hole in his gut to watch her up there with Charlie. At least Travis would have an excuse to feast his eyes on her for a little while.

"How's she doing?" He was unable to keep himself from voicing the question.

"She looks the same as you," Adam replied "Tired and troubled." He glanced at Travis. "Only thing is, on her even that looks good."

The night of the pageant was cold and clear, the snow on the ground frozen to a sheet of silver that sparkled in the moonlight. Rory had expected to ride with Charlie, Adam and Kim, but Mrs. Clark wanted to go, as well as a friend of Kim's who was spending the night, so Travis picked her up in his truck.

"Are you nervous about singing?" he asked, breaking the silence that had descended between them like a smothering velvet curtain. "You said once that you weren't used to performing."

"I'm terrified," she confessed, gripping her hands together to stop their shaking. "I've never sung in public, and I don't know how I let Charlie talk me into this." She was wearing a slim dark blue dress that matched her eyes, and she could have sworn it was tighter around the waist than the last time she'd worn it. Her breasts were fuller, and she wondered if Travis had noticed when he'd helped her with her coat.

"You look very nice," he said politely, glancing in her direction.

She'd pinned up her hair, but already some of the shorter strands had worked their way loose to tickle her neck. What if it all came undone right in the middle of their song? What if her voice quit on her or she forgot the words?

"Turn the truck around," she said suddenly, yanking on his arm. "I can't do this."

"What?" Travis pulled away from her grasp. "You aren't serious."

"Oh, I am," she wailed as nerves threatened to thoroughly swamp her composure. "I was a fool to agree. I can't go through with it." She was starting to babble, hysteria rising in her throat. "I want to go home. Charlie can sing without me."

"Why did you agree to it if you feel this way?" Travis asked.

Rory was too bent on convincing him to turn around to pay much attention to his question. "I don't know," she moaned. "Because Charlie asked me to, I guess, and to make you jealous." As soon as the words were out, she realized what she'd admitted.

Travis glanced at her, and then he pulled off the road, bouncing over the frozen ruts to the shoulder where he parked the truck.

"You want to run that by me again?" he asked, voice dangerously soft.

Now he had Rory's full attention. Her panic ebbed away, replaced by acute embarrassment. Biting her lower lip, she tried to think of a plausible explanation for what she'd let slip, but her only option was to brazen it out.

"I never meant for you and Charlie to come to blows," she said hastily. "I was lonesome, and I just wanted you to pay a little more attention to me. That's all there ever was to it, I swear.''

Carefully, Travis wrapped his fingers around the steering wheel. ''That's all? You're sure?''

''Please, would you just take me back to the house?'' she asked, ignoring his question. Her stomach had begun to churn alarmingly, and she didn't want to be sick by the side of the road—or at the church. ''I don't feel well. I can't possibly sing tonight. Please?''

Travis pulled back on the road, but he didn't turn around. Instead, he headed down the highway toward what Rory was sure would be her next humiliating experience of the evening.

A car passed them going the other way, and then Travis surprised her by taking her trembling hand in his. ''If you get nervous,'' he said, squeezing it gently, ''maybe it would help if you look right at my face. Forget everyone else and sing to me. Just to me. Think you can do that?''

''I don't know.'' She was stunned by his suggestion. ''I guess I could try.'' Would it work? Could she do it? It would sure beat letting Charlie down when he'd practiced so hard on the duet. Slowly her nerves began to quiet.

''Travis?'' she murmured, tugging on his hand. She wanted to ask him why he was helping her.

Headlights were coming toward them, and there was a bridge up ahead. He glanced at her and smiled. ''What?''

The oncoming lights shifted, blinding her.

''Travis!'' Rory shouted a warning. The other vehicle was headed straight at them.

The bridge was far too icy for him to hit the brakes. He tried to steer around the oncoming truck, but it was too far over the center line.

"Brace yourself," he shouted, cranking the wheel as the other truck, a big one, plowed into them and smashed them against the bridge railing. Rory heard the wood splinter and scrape on impact. Metal shrieked a protest.

For a moment there was nothing but an odd creaking noise. Time stopped. They were weightless, their headlights stabbing the darkness as the world around them spun. The dash lights glowed eerily as they tipped.

Travis flung out his arm to hold her. "Dammit, we're going over. Hang on to me."

They were falling through the dark, and then there was a huge splash. Rory was flung forward, a rushing sound in her ears, and the seat belt bit into her stomach.

"The baby!" she cried, and then her head snapped back.

"Where am I?" Her voice was faint, and her face was the color of old ivory, but her eyes were finally open.

"Thank God." Holding tight to her hand, Travis struggled against the dry lump in his throat as relief surged through him. Tears welled in his eyes, but he blinked them away, figuring they'd only scare her.

In the ambulance, she'd drifted in and out of consciousness. There was a lump on her head and she had a few bruises, but it could have been so much worse.

"You're in the hospital," he told her, shifting the blanket wrapped around his shoulders. "You're going to be fine." The emergency staff had determined she had no internal bleeding or broken bones. So far, the baby seemed okay. He hadn't even dealt with that yet. At first he'd thought he heard her wrong, but the doctor who examined her confirmed it after Travis told her what Rory had said.

Now the doctor came into the cubicle, introduced herself to Rory, who was still blinking owlishly, and shone a light in her eyes. "Everything looks okay," the doctor said, smiling. "Mother and baby are both doing well." She tucked a strand of gray hair behind one ear and put her hand in the pocket of her white coat.

"You were in an accident," she told Rory. "Your truck went off a bridge into the water and you have a nasty bump on your head, but that's all. If your husband hadn't pulled you out, you might have drowned."

It had been so black, Travis remembered with a shudder. The river wasn't deep, but at first he hadn't been able to find her in the darkness. Then he saw the pale oval of her face under the water and his heart nearly stopped. By the time he got her seat belt free and hauled her to the surface, helping hands were there to drag them both to the bank. He'd nearly passed out from the pain.

Someone had a lantern and blankets. Travis hadn't even noticed the freezing cold as Rory coughed out the water she'd swallowed. All he felt was her clammy hand in his, as cool as death.

Rory was looking up at him now, her eyes clouded

and her hair a tangled mess. "Are you okay?" she asked.

"I'm fine," he said huskily. Inside he was still shaking. Everything had happened so quickly, the feed truck skidding out of control. He'd barely had time to react.

Rory looked at the doctor. "Is he telling the truth? Is he all right?"

"He's as strong as a bull. Even with a dislocated shoulder, he managed to pull you from the wreck." A smile etched deep lines into her worn cheeks. "This one's a keeper, honey. I'd hang on to him if I were you."

Rory glanced at Travis and back to the doctor. "And the baby?" she asked.

"Right as rain." She gave them both some quick instructions and then she left, promising to come back later.

"The rest of the family's in the waiting room," Travis said. They needed to talk, but now wasn't the time. "Adam went back to get us both some dry clothes. I'm sure they'll want to see you if you're up to it."

"In a minute," she murmured, capturing his hand. "As soon as I thank you for saving my life." She tugged him closer. Travis yielded easily, bending to plant a careful kiss on her mouth. When her lips parted beneath his, he jerked upward.

She wrapped her hand around his neck. "I won't break," she said. "Dr. Ames promised."

He searched her eyes, and all the strain of the last hour came flooding back. He could have lost her. Cradling her head with care, he poured his heart into a long, hungry kiss.

Rory couldn't believe they were back at square one, not after what they'd been through, not after the way Travis had acted at the hospital.

"He's like a stranger," she complained to Charlie as he sat beside her on the couch. She had wanted to go straight home from the hospital, but Travis had insisted she stay at Adam's for a couple of days so Mrs. Clark could keep an eye on her. It wasn't Mrs. Clark who Rory wanted fussing over her, but Travis had only come to see her twice.

"He seemed pleased about the baby," she added. "He asked when I was due and whether I'd seen a doctor besides the one at the hospital." She'd thought the news might bring them closer. Instead, he'd withdrawn again. When she had tried to thank him for saving her, he'd even acted angry, puzzling her further.

"Give him a little more time," Charlie suggested. "He must have gone through sheer hell until he found you in the river. It was pitch-black when we got there. The only part of the truck I could even see from the bridge was the headlights." Adam's car had been a few minutes behind them on the road. Charlie claimed Rory had apologized for messing up their number, but she didn't remember a thing.

Quite a few members of the congregation had called to see how she was, but the housekeeper had fielded the calls. The pastor stopped by, as did the choir director, Mr. Stanley, and several women who brought food, but none of them had lingered. When

Kim was home from school, she hovered, ready to fetch anything Rory wanted.

"Travis and I have wasted enough time," she told Charlie. She was going back home today if she had to walk. "I want my husband. I've hardly seen him. He asks how I am and whether I need anything, then he disappears as though he's scared to death of me."

"He *is* scared," Charlie said. "He almost lost you, and he's had to face his own feelings about you. He'll come around."

"I'm moving back to the house," she said. "Will you take me?"

Charlie frowned. "Thanksgiving's in three days. Why don't you stay here till then?"

Rory's mind was made up. "No. I feel fine. Travis has brooded long enough. If I wait, he'll have to get used to me all over again. With or without your help, I'm going back now."

"Okay," Charlie agreed with a sigh. "He and Adam are out on the range today, but I'm not sure where. If you're so determined, why don't you get your stuff together."

"I'm all packed and my tote bag is in the guest room," Rory said, rising. She picked up the tray the housekeeper had brought her earlier, with a stack of magazines and the television remote. "I want to thank Mrs. Clark for all her help and then I'll be ready to go."

"Adam will have my head for this," Charlie mumbled unhappily as he went up the stairs for her bag. "If Travis doesn't kill me first."

When Travis pulled up behind his house that evening after he'd eaten with the men, he was surprised to see light pouring from the windows. Perhaps Mrs. Clark had come by and left them on. He hoped she hadn't brought him dinner; he'd feel guilty if she'd gone to the trouble.

Slamming the door of his truck, he walked through the snow that had started falling lightly. His boots crunched across the frozen ground. The house looked so welcoming, lit up against the night, that he almost wished he didn't have to change and go to Adam's.

He knew he'd been neglecting Rory since the accident, but he couldn't seem to help himself. Coming so close to losing her had ripped away the scab he'd kept over his feelings, leaving them raw and exposed. Each time he saw her was like probing the wound with a stick. He felt cornered, trapped by his own vulnerability, and now there was a baby to think about. His baby. The idea filled him with both terror and joy. He stood to lose even more than before.

He hung up his hat and coat, and then he went into the kitchen. Someone had made coffee. Grateful, he got out a mug and poured a shot of the dark, steaming brew.

When he visited Rory tonight, he planned to ask her to come back and make a real marriage with him. It no longer mattered if he choked, groping for the right words, and ended up looking like a pathetic fool. It only mattered that she knew he loved her. He owed her that.

The whole idea sent a shiver of dread through him, and his hand shook, spilling coffee onto the floor. Grumbling, he grabbed a sponge from the sink and bent down to wipe up the drips. When he started to straighten, he saw a pair of feet in the doorway.

Bare feet with painted toes. Slowly, Travis raised his gaze, which traveled up bare legs that went on forever and stopped at a lacy turquoise teddy that covered a lovely feminine form.

Rory was posed against the doorjamb and no clue of her recent ordeal showed. Her breasts swelled above the neckline of her outfit, but her waist was as slim as ever. Her peach-tinted lips were curved into a smile of welcome, and her darkened lashes fluttered. She looked more beautiful than he'd ever seen her.

While Travis swallowed and tried to find his voice, she padded slowly across the kitchen, her hips swaying and her gaze locked on his. Her sweet, sultry scent made his head spin and clouded his thoughts. Stopping in front of him, she reached up and gently traced a finger down his cheek.

''Hi.'' Her voice was husky.

His lungs emptied; his heart thudded. ''What are you doing here?'' he croaked. ''I thought you were at Adam's.'' His gaze roved from the top of her head to her toes and back. ''You need rest.''

''I need you,'' she corrected him gently.

''Me?'' His voice cracked like a schoolboy's. Heat ran up his cheeks. What was she playing at?

She took his hand and tugged playfully. ''Come with me,'' she coaxed.

Travis thought about protesting, considered demanding they talk first, let his gaze wander from her lush mouth to her creamy curves, sucked in more of her scent, and returned her smile with a helpless grin of his own.

He could no more deny her than he could deny the love welling up inside him like Texas crude. "Lead the way," he said, setting his mug on the counter. "I'm right behind you."

Chapter Thirteen

Breathless with anticipation and nerves, Rory led Travis to the stairs. Her foot was on the bottom step when she felt him resist. She looked back at him, so tall in his boots next to her bare feet.

"I missed you," he said. "Welcome home." He dipped his head and pressed a kiss to her mouth.

"I missed you, too." She lifted her hand and cradled his jaw as she studied his strong, attractive face. Why hadn't she realized the truth before?

He loved her. She was sure of it. He'd risked his life to save hers. Fighting for the one you loved could take many forms. He'd fought to keep her alive, and now it was her turn. After what they'd been through, standing on pride seemed a little silly.

Rory was about to lay hers at her husband's feet.

"What about the baby?" he asked when she started up the stairs.

His concern reminded her what a good man he was. "The baby will be fine," she assured him. "I checked with Dr. Ames back at the hospital while you were getting dressed. Normal activities are okay."

A muscle in his jaw flexed, and then he curved an arm around her shoulders. "Normal activities, huh?" There was a hint of laughter in his eyes as well as swirling desire. "Could you give me an example of what might be considered a normal activity?"

Rory pretended to think. "Horseback riding, dancing, pulling weeds."

"In November?"

"Well, probably not," she conceded. "Maybe walking in the snow instead."

"How about vacuuming, housework, laundry?" he asked.

She gave him a mock frown. "I don't think so."

He leaned closer. "Making love?" he whispered in her ear.

"Why, sir," she teased, fluttering her eyelashes. "Is that a proposition?"

Travis nuzzled her ear, his breath against her neck sending shivers of reaction all through her. "A request," he murmured. "A plea from a desperate man. Call it whatever you want. The truth of the matter is that I've missed you."

Rory's heart melted. "I've missed you, too." Oh, how she wanted to pour out her feelings, but caution stilled her tongue. First she wanted to lie in his arms and let herself believe he loved her as much as she did him. Breath coming fast and shallow, she led him up the stairs.

Before he'd gotten home, she'd made up the bed

with fresh linens, turned down the covers and lit a few scented candles. Now she worried that she might have gone overboard, but her fears were instantly put to rest when he stopped in the doorway and his arm tightened around her.

"This is nice." He skimmed his hand down her side and turned her gently to him. "Perhaps it can be a new start for us," he added hoarsely.

"I'd like that." Rory was eager to discuss the idea, but not now. Ever since the accident, she'd been reassessing her life. Now she wanted to reaffirm it. Travis's nearness, his kisses and the touch of his hand on her skin all fueled her desire. The last thing she wanted right now was to talk.

Boldly, she reached up and began unsnapping his shirt. He stood still, letting her tug the long tail free of his jeans. Beneath it, he wore a thermal undershirt, which she also yanked loose, and then she burrowed her hands beneath the hem. His skin was hot and smooth. She caressed his back, savoring the feel of him, and then she brought her hand around to his chest. The crisp hairs tickled her palms and his nipples peaked against her fingertips.

Travis's breath caught, and a shudder rippled through him. His hands tightened on her upper arms, and he bent to nibble her shoulder. Rory angled her head, and he slid down the strap of her teddy. His mouth was hot, his tongue seeking out all the sensitive little hollows along the base of her throat.

He slipped down her other strap, and she caught the front of the teddy before it could slip. Travis stepped back and stripped off his shirt. His undershirt followed. As he pulled it over his head, Rory watched the muscles in his chest and arms flex and shift. He was powerfully built; her mouth went dry.

Bared to the waist, he let his gaze drop to where her hands were holding her teddy against her breasts. His brows rose in silent query. It was as if he'd cast aside all the stresses between them, focusing totally on what was taking place right now in this room.

A new start, she realized. With a teasing smile, she let her hands drop. Slowly the teddy slithered downward and ended in a splash of turquoise at her feet.

While Travis watched her through narrowed eyes, Rory stepped over the discarded teddy and moved closer to the bed.

"You're so beautiful." His voice was thick with desire, and his obvious approval dispelled the last shreds of her self-consciousness.

Rory leaned forward and trailed kisses across his chest. "So are you," she murmured against his skin. His heart thundered beneath her lips. He buried his hands in her hair and tipped back her head.

This hot-blooded melding of mouths was raw, wanton and carnal. His lips moved on hers with an urgency that fired her blood. His tongue thrust inside, caressing her with greedy strokes. His hands found her breasts.

Arching her back, she pressed her hips closer, and the cold metal of his buckle kissed her stomach. She wrapped her fingers around his wide leather belt.

"This has to go," she told him, tugging lightly. Then she scraped her nails down the line of hair that dipped beneath his jeans. His stomach quivered and his breath hissed out. He surprised her by chuckling.

"First the boots," he reminded her, sitting on the

edge of the bed to remove them and his socks. Next he dealt with his belt and jeans. He slanted a look at her and then he removed his shorts. Grabbing Rory, he fell backward on the bed. She landed sprawled across him. He rolled, holding her, so she ended up underneath him.

Tenderly, hungrily, urgently, Travis caressed her until she hummed with tension. Desire bubbled in her veins like champagne. By the time he parted her thighs and slid into her, she was moaning with need. At his first thrust, she cried out his name. Ruthlessly, he drove her up and over, barely giving her time to catch her breath before he began again. This time, when she peaked, her body shattering, he was with her all the way.

When Rory awakened, the candles were out, the room was dark, and Travis lay sleeping beside her. His arm anchored her close, and her hand was spread across his chest. She could barely make out his profile in the gloom.

Gathering her courage, she propped herself carefully up on one elbow. "I love you," she murmured.

He didn't stir. His breathing remained steady, his body relaxed. Poor man, he was worn-out. Her confession of love would have to wait. Smiling, she lay back down and cuddled close, thrusting one leg over his as she absorbed his warmth and his nearness.

When she woke again, she was in the same position, but she had an urgent need to get up. He didn't move, but when she came back from the bathroom, shivering in the cold, she could see that his eyes were open.

"Are you feeling okay?" he asked.

"Mm-hm." He lifted the edge of the sheet, and she slid in beside him. The bed was a toasty nest. "Sorry I woke you."

"I'm not," he said in a throaty purr as he turned on his side. His desire set fire to her own as his hands blazed a trail. This time when they joined, she straddled him, her hands braced on his chest as she set the pace.

"Rory, honey, I can't wait," he gasped as his body went taut beneath her. His hands tightened on her hips as he bucked. His body arched and he surged against her. She felt him convulse, heard his harsh groan of fulfillment. Before he was done, satisfaction rolled through her like a tidal wave. When it was over, she collapsed against him.

"I love you," she gasped.

Beneath her, he went still.

"What did you say?" he demanded.

It was easier the second time. She lifted her head and smiled into the darkness. "I said that I love you," she repeated softly. "I'm sorry I haven't told you until now. I can't keep it to myself any longer."

Nearly dumping her over, he reached up and snapped on the light beside the bed. There was a blinding flash, and Rory squeezed her eyes shut. "Oh, why did you do that?"

He shifted away from her. At first she thought he was going to leave, and her heart plummeted. Her eyes popped open, and she realized he'd pulled himself to a sitting position and was staring at her intently.

"Now that I can see you, would you mind repeating what you just said?'' he asked. ''I want to see your eyes when you say it.''

''My eyes?'' Rory echoed, confused by his reaction. ''Why?''

His smile, when it came, was crooked and infinitely sweet. ''I never dreamed I'd ever see love in your eyes,'' he confessed raggedly. ''I see it there now.''

Rory's heart overflowed with a wave of tenderness. Here was a man who'd lived with a shortage of affection since he'd lost his mother. His father hadn't been demonstrative. He'd been too busy building a ranching empire. When was the last time anyone had told Travis they loved him?

Sitting up beside him, she reached out a hand and caressed his cheek. His whiskers rasped against her skin. She looked deep into his eyes and smiled.

''It's been in my eyes for you to see for quite a while,'' she said softly. ''I've loved you almost since the very beginning.''

His brows furrowed. ''Why?'' he asked. ''Why would you love me?''

''Don't you know how dear and sweet you are?'' She wanted to cry for his uncertainty.

He colored and jerked away from her hand. Determined, she laid it back against his cheek and turned his head gently around back to face her. ''I'm not leaving,'' she said. ''You can't drive me away. I love you, I love the ranch, and I love your baby growing inside me. Those are the facts, Winchester, and they aren't going to change, so deal with them.''

Heart pounding, she waited for him to say something, anything, in response to her challenge. She hadn't meant to go on like that, but once she got started, the words just seemed to tumble out. Poor man, her declaration had probably scared him speechless.

For a moment, he merely stared, his expression unreadable. Then, as she started to panic, afraid she'd misjudged him and he didn't care for her after all, he squeezed his eyes shut.

A single tear rolled down his weathered cheek. "I love you," he whispered raggedly, hands fisting at his sides. "You have no idea how much."

Rory threw her arms around his neck. "I hoped," she babbled, "but I wasn't sure. Sometimes I thought yes, and sometimes no." She hugged him tight as his arms came around her like steel bands.

"I was afraid to love you," he mumbled against her shoulder. "If I lost you—"

"Sh, don't talk like that." She caressed his hair, kissed his cheek, touched him wherever she could reach. "I'm not going anywhere."

He straightened, his smile crooked and his eyes shining with happiness she realized she was responsible for putting there. Sometimes a person had to take a chance.

"After the other night," he said, "I didn't know what to do. It was as though my feelings had broken loose. I thought if I stayed away from you for a little while, I could get them back under control."

He swallowed, licked his lips. Rory squeezed his hand but she stayed quiet, sensing there were things he had to get out.

"It wasn't working," he admitted with a rueful smile. "Tonight when I came home and found you here, I'd been trying to figure out how to tell you.'' Abruptly, maddeningly, he fell silent.

''Tell me what?'' she demanded impatiently.

His smile widened. ''Tell you that I adore you, I can't live without you, and you'd better get used to Colorado, because it's going to be your home for a very long time.''

''How long?'' Rory asked tremulously, basking in the love she could see on his face.

Travis kissed the back of her hand. ''For as long as we both shall live.''

* * * * *

The Winning Hand

here was something wonderfully smooth under her
eek. Silk, satin, Darcy thought dimly. She'd always loved
e feel of silk. Once she'd spent nearly her entire paycheck
a silk blouse, creamy white with gold, heart shaped but-
ns. She'd had to skip lunch for two weeks, but it had
en worth it every time she slipped that silk over her skin.
She sighed, remembering it.
"Come on, all the way out."
"What?" She blinked her eyes open, focused on a slant
light from a jeweled lamp.
"Here, try this." Mac slipped a hand under her head,
ted it, and put a glass of water to her lips.
"What?"
"You're repeating yourself. Drink some water."
"Okay." She sipped obediently, studying the tanned,
ng-fingered hand that held the glass. She was on a bed,
e realized now, a huge bed with a silky cover. There was

a mirrored ceiling over her head. “Oh my.” Warily, sh
shifted her gaze until she saw his face.

He set the glass aside, then sat on the edge of the be
noting with amusement that she scooted over slightly t
keep more distance between them. “Mac Blade. I run th
place.”

“Darcy. I’m Darcy Wallace. Why am I here?”

“It seemed better than leaving you sprawled on the flo
of the casino. You fainted.”

“I did?” Mortified, she closed her eyes again. “Yes,
guess I did. I’m sorry.”

“It’s not an atypical reaction to winning close to tw
million dollars.”

Her eyes popped open, her hand grabbed at her thro
“I’m sorry. I’m still a little confused. Did you say I wo
almost two million dollars?”

“You put the money in, you pulled the lever, you hit
There wasn’t an ounce of color in her cheeks, he note
and thought she looked like a bruised fairy. “Do you wa
to see a doctor?”

“No, I’m just…I’m okay. I can’t think. My head’s spi
ning.”

“Take your time.” Instinctively, he plumped up the p
lows behind her and eased her back.

“I had nine dollars and thirty-seven cents when I g
here.”

“Well, now you have $1 800 088.37.”

“Oh. Oh.” Shattered, she put her hands over her fa
and burst into tears.

There were too many women in his life for Mac to
uncomfortable with female tears. He sat where he was a
let her sob it out.

“I’m sorry.” She wiped her hands at her someh
charmingly dirty face. “I’m not like this. Really. I ca
take it in.” She accepted the handkerchief he offered a
blew her nose. “I don’t know what to do.”

"Let's start with the basics. Why don't you take a hot ath, try to relax, get your bearings. There's a robe in the loset."

She cleared her throat. However kind he was being, she vas still alone with him, a perfect stranger, in a very op-ılent and sensual bedroom. "I appreciate it. But I should get a room. If I could have a small advance on the money, can find a hotel."

"Something wrong with this one?"

"This what?"

"This hotel," he said. "This room."

"No, nothing. It's beautiful."

"Then make yourself comfortable. Your room's been omped for the duration of your stay—"

"What? Excuse me?" She sat up a little straighter. "I an have this room? I can just…stay here?"

"It's the usual procedure for high rollers." He smiled gain, making her heart bump. "You qualify."

"I get all this for free because I won money from you?"

His grin was quick, and just a little wolfish. "I want the hance to win some of it back."

Lord, he was beautiful. Like the hero of a novel. That hought rolled around in her jumbled brain. "That seems nly fair. Thank you so much, Mr. Blade."

"Welcome to Las Vegas, Ms. Wallace," he said and ırned toward a sweep of open stairs that led to the living rea.

She watched him cross an ocean of Oriental carpet. "Mr. lade?"

"Yes?" He turned and glanced up.

"What will I do with all that money?"

He flashed that grin again. "You'll think of something."

When the doors closed behind him, Darcy gave into her ıckling knees and sat on the floor. She hugged herself ard, rocking back and forth. If this was some dream, some hallucination brought on by stress or sunstroke, she hoped it never cleared away.

She hadn't just escaped her life, she realized. She'd been liberated.

COMING NEXT MONTH

TEMPORARY DADDY Jennifer Mikels

That's My Baby!

Marriage, let alone fatherhood, was never an option for bachelor Dylan Marek, which was why he had run a mile when he fell for Chelsea Huntsford. Now Chelsea was back with a baby boy. Could he be Dylan's?

HEART OF THE HUNTER Lindsay McKenna

Morgan's Mercenaries

Captain Reid Hunter had sacrificed a personal life for the sake of his military career, and no woman could penetrate his steely heart—until he met Dr Casey Morrow. His mission was to protect her, but was he the one in need of protection—from love?

A HERO FOR SOPHIE JONES Christine Rimmer

The Jones Gang

Revenge by seduction was Sinclair Riker's objective and Sophie Jones was his intended victim! But there was something about Sophie's sweet kisses that drove all thoughts of vengeance from Sin's mind. Could Sophie turn Sin into a saint?

A FAMILY KIND OF GUY Lisa Jackson

At eighteen Bliss Cawthorne had been determined to marry Mason Lafferty, but her father had intervened, and Mason married another. Ten years later Bliss is back, and Mason, now a single father, is not about to let her go again!

EVERY COWGIRL'S DREAM Arlene James

To inherit her family ranch, Kara Detmeyer had been set the challenge of her life. She had to drive a herd of cattle hundreds of miles, *and* she had to do it with Rye Wagner, the moodiest, most gorgeous man she'd ever met.

DIAGNOSIS: DADDY Jule McBride

Big Apple Babies

Francesca Luccetti had a problem because, although she desperately wanted a baby, she neither had, nor wanted, a husband! An adoption agency seemed the answer—but the agency's handsome doctor, 'Doc' Holiday, had other ideas…